## ACKNOWLEDGMENT

All authors try to be as accurate as possible; nevertheless, in order to tell a story, fictional liberties are often taken. I'm certainly no exception in this regard. However, Title VII is real, and violations of this civil rights law are illegal in the United States, where workers have the right to a harassment- and discrimination-free workplace. For more information, please visit www.eeoc.gov, or call 1-800-669-4000.

A special thank-you goes to Dwayne Swacker, Spanish teacher at Francis Howell High School, for his language expertise. Any errors in his work are mine.

Dear Reader,

There is no such thing as a normal life. But that's not about to stop Christina Jones from searching for it. She's not interested in the sexy volunteer firefighter who saves the day at her daughter's elementary school, especially once she learns he's the man whose day job involves the law firm where she's just taken on a senior partnership. And Christina doesn't need another "prince"—she's already had that experience! As for Bruce Lancaster, firefighter/whiz lawyer, he's about to discover that love comes in unexpected packages, and that to rescue his own heart, he may need to go above and beyond the call of duty.

For my tenth book, I wanted to write about those firefighters who lay their hearts and lives on the line every day, especially the ones who volunteer for the job and serve rural communities like mine. Setting the story close to my cousins' home gave me an excuse to visit again.

I hope you enjoy reading about Christina and Bruce as much as I did writing them. They are very close to my heart. As always, feel free to e-mail me at michele@micheledunaway.com, and be sure to look for Olivia Jacobsen's story later this year. You'll remember her as Shane's sister from *About Last Night....*

Enjoy the romance!

*Michele Dunaway*

# LEGALLY TENDER
## MICHELE DUNAWAY

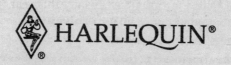

HARLEQUIN®

TORONTO • NEW YORK • LONDON
AMSTERDAM • PARIS • SYDNEY • HAMBURG
STOCKHOLM • ATHENS • TOKYO • MILAN • MADRID
PRAGUE • WARSAW • BUDAPEST • AUCKLAND

ISBN 0-373-75104-4

LEGALLY TENDER

For the McMenamy family, who welcomed me as their own, especially John Michael and Lucy Kate. I am very proud of both of you and what you have done with your lives.

And to the staff at Francis Howell High School. Thanks for letting me work with such great people.

## Books by Michele Dunaway

**HARLEQUIN AMERICAN ROMANCE**

848—A LITTLE OFFICE ROMANCE
900—TAMING THE TABLOID HEIRESS
921—THE SIMPLY SCANDALOUS PRINCESS
931—CATCHING THE CORPORATE PLAYBOY
963—SWEEPING THE BRIDE AWAY
988—THE PLAYBOY'S PROTÉGÉE
1008—ABOUT LAST NIGHT…
1044—UNWRAPPING MR. WRIGHT
1056—EMERGENCY ENGAGEMENT

Don't miss any of our special offers. Write to us at the following address for information on our newest releases.

Harlequin Reader Service
U.S.: 3010 Walden Ave., P.O. Box 1325, Buffalo, NY 14269
Canadian: P.O. Box 609, Fort Erie, Ont. L2A 5X3

# Chapter One

She had never felt so incompetent in her life. It was her fault the thick gray smoke billowed, the fire alarms blared and the fire trucks honked obnoxiously in the distance.

This time it wasn't because she'd burned the Thanksgiving turkey. No. This time she'd ruined Halloween.

Her eyes watered as the acrid smoke traveled from the large gym into the elementary-school cafeteria. She could almost hear her ex-husband's condescending voice over the clanging fire-alarm bells: "Christina Sanchez Jones, when will you learn to do something right?" And yet Christina had graduated with honors from prestigious Harvard Law School.

"Mama? Are you crying?" a tiny voice asked as the harsh bells finally ceased.

Christina blinked and glanced down at her eight-year-old daughter. Bella sported black cat whiskers. A beaded black headband complete with furry black-and-pink cat ears held her dark-blond hair away from her face. "We won't have to cancel the Halloween party, will we, Mama? There wasn't a fire. Only fake smoke."

"No," Christina said, wiping the back of her left hand across her eyes. Through the cafeteria windows, Christina could see that a fire truck had pulled into the parking lot. "We are not canceling. We still have bobbing for apples and a craft left to do. We just won't have the haunted house."

"That's okay! I don't care!" Bella shouted. She turned back to the other second-grade members of her Brownie troop. Like Bella, they were dressed in Halloween costumes. "The party's still on!" she whooped.

"Why don't you all go eat your snacks," Christina suggested as a group of firemen raced through the cafeteria into the gym. Their heavy boots thudded on the freshly buffed floor. "Mrs. Sims," Christina called, "let's do snack now. Does that sound good?"

"Absolutely," Mrs. Sims replied. Darla Sims was an unofficial troop leader, and within seconds, she had all the girls organized at a cafeteria table, eating pumpkin-shaped cookies and drinking witches' brew—a concoction of orange juice, lime sherbet and white soda pop.

Christina sighed and entered the gym. The firemen were checking out what was to have been a haunted house.

There really hadn't been a fire, but Christina should have known better. She should have realized that a smoke machine would not only create a spooky atmosphere, but it would also trigger the smoke detectors and, in turn, the school's fire-alarm system. She'd known exactly what was happening the moment the first fire bell pealed. Now her mother's voice resounded in Christina's head. The good woman had supported Christina's divorce from Kyle Jones, but she hadn't wanted her daughter to move to Morrisville, Indiana. Too Midwest, too far from Houston, too small town and simply too far from home and the myriad of relatives who lived just a short plane ride over the Mexican border. "If you're such a hotshot lawyer," her mother had argued, "you should have been able to get around that seventy-five-mile child-custody restriction in your divorce decree. You should have been allowed to move anywhere. Like home. Morrisville, Indiana? Do they even have a McDonald's in that town?"

The answer was yes. Morrisville did have the fast-food restaurant, right at the Highway 74 overpass and next to the town's new gas station—

A deep voice cut through her turbulent thoughts. "They said you were the one in charge."

Actually, the woman in charge of the Brownie troop's Friday-night Halloween party was home with the flu. Her directions had included plugging in the smoke machine. But that didn't give Christina an excuse. One of her role models was law-school graduate and thirty-third president of the United States, Harry S. Truman. To paraphrase Truman, *The buck stopped with her.*

Prepared to accept full responsibility, she turned and looked behind her.

And into the clearest blue eyes she'd ever seen. She

resisted her instinct to step back, and took a deep breath. "I'm in charge," she admitted.

"So you're responsible for this?" The fireman made a wide sweeping gesture with his right hand, his serious gaze holding hers.

"Yes," she replied as her breath lodged in her throat.

He had to be six-foot-one, only a smidgen shorter than her ex-husband, Kyle. As the firefighter continued to stare at her, Christina shifted under his appraisal.

She knew exactly what he saw: skin the color of a light suntan, hair the color of ripened wheat, brown eyes with a hint of gold, and a genie costume complete with exposed midriff and curled blue shoes that were fast causing her feet to ache. At five foot nine, she was model tall, and she'd long ago accepted that she was the nonstereotypical one in her Mexican family. She didn't have the cliché dark hair and dark skin. Instead, her lighter hair and skin came from genes dating back to the time of Cortez, and intermingling of Spanish and Aztec blood.

She regained her composure. She'd dealt with being labeled incompetent and second rate long enough. She'd lived with not meeting anyone's expectations, and she'd determined that, with her move to Morrisville, the only ones she had to live with now were her own.

She was a take-charge woman at this point in her life, in control of her own mistakes and her own destiny. She would lace on metaphorical boxing gloves and step into the ring with anyone who wanted to teach her otherwise.

She lifted her chin slightly to answer the attractive

firefighter who waited impatiently. "Yes, I'm the one who plugged in the smoke machine. As soon as the alarm went off, I knew why. I guess the lady who left me directions for setting up the party thought the gym ceiling was high enough."

"It wasn't."

"Obviously," Christina said dryly. She would not let this college-age boy affect her or her newfound empowerment. However, as he took off his black helmet, she saw he was much older than she'd thought. Late twenties, perhaps, judging from laugh lines that weren't showing any amusement at the moment. *But if he smiled....*

The man shrugged out of his firefighter's coat. Underneath he was wearing a long-sleeved navy Morrisville Fire Department T-shirt. Suspenders held up his black firefighter pants. The man's muscular build indicated he was a strong believer in physical fitness. Bodies were something Christina noticed—especially after having been married to a professional football player whose body was his life. The man in front of her wasn't bulky enough to play pro football, but the hard, lean lines of his physique communicated innate strength.

The helmet had flattened the firefighter's dark-brown hair. Now he tousled the strands with his free hand. "We'll use fans to air out the gym and cafeteria and clear away any residual smoke. That's about all we can do. You'll need to clean the rest up yourselves," he said.

"We will," Christina promised.

He shook his head, obviously still disgusted by her foolish mistake. He moved aside as a member of his crew carried in a huge steel fan and proceeded to set it up on the floor by the gym exit door. "You'll also need to leave the outside doors open. Luckily for you, it's unseasonably warm tonight. It won't get too cold in here."

"Yes," Christina said. She glanced down as a small hand tugged on hers.

"We want to see the fire truck," Bella said hopefully, speaking for her friends. "Please, Mama?"

Christina shot the firefighter an apologetic look. Children, she tried to tell him. "Honey, he's busy, and you should not be in here."

"I'm never too busy for a group of kids," the firefighter said, surprising Christina. He finally cracked a smile, one so endearing she suddenly wished he could have directed it at her, too, instead of only at Bella. "Come on, now that all you little girls have got us out here, you must see the fire truck."

"Do you live at the firehouse?" Bella asked as she followed him, her long black cat tail swishing behind her.

"Nope," the man said as the Brownie troop gathered around him. "We're all volunteers. We come from our homes whenever we get the call that someone needs us."

"The smoke machine set off the alarm," announced Megan, the girl who had become Bella's best friend.

"And that's why we're here," he said with another large smile. "Now, walk around this big fan—careful now—and you can all see the fire truck."

The firefighter's grin widened, revealing straight white teeth. It was a Dennis Quaid smile, Christina decided, like in *The Parent Trap* or *The Rookie*. She'd watched both films recently with Bella. The grin, complete with dimples, covered the firefighter's entire face. A lifetime ago he might have been her type, she thought wistfully.

The Brownie troop dutifully followed him outside, past the circular fan. Careful not to bump into it herself, Christina hovered at the door as several firefighters began to show the girls the equipment on the fire truck.

"Well, that'll keep them occupied for a bit," Mrs. Sims commented as she approached.

"Yes," Christina said, her gaze never leaving the scene in the parking lot. "Even though it appears everything's okay, I should probably go out there and supervise."

"That sounds wise. I'll get the crafts set up. The girls are pretty much finished eating. At least one thing will go right tonight. I don't know what Lula was thinking. A smoke machine."

"What a fiasco," Christina agreed.

"Mistakes happen to the best of us. Don't worry, Christina, those guys get called out of their homes all the time and at all hours. They know it when they sign up to volunteer."

"Volunteer?"

"Yes." Mrs. Sims's brow creased for only a second. "I forgot that you're not from here. Morrisville's fire department is an all-volunteer force. No one's paid. Even Batesville's fire department is entirely volunteer, and Batesville is a much larger town that's home to a Fortune 1000 company."

Christina winced. She hadn't realized that volunteer fire departments still existed. Actually, up until two weeks ago, she hadn't realized quaint little rural communities like Morrisville, population 4,231, still existed. When she'd first interviewed with the law firm of Lancaster and Morris, she'd received a tour of the place, but it had lasted all of ten minutes—the time it took to drive from the Highway 74 exit, through the town square, to the farms on the other side of town.

"Most people around here who aren't farmers work ten miles away in Batesville at one of the Hillenbrand Industries," Reginald Morris, the senior partner, had told Christina during the tour. "There are several other smaller manufacturing companies in the area, but none with a large output. We're hiring you for the case against the Morrisville Garment Company, a small company located just on the outskirts of our town. A Title VII class-action suit is being brought on behalf of a group of Hispanic women, mostly of Mexican descent. One priority for our success in this harassment case is having a partner who can speak Spanish and relate to our clients."

"That's a task I'm ready for," Christina had replied. As a Hispanic female herself, she was drawn by the opportunity to help those women. They belonged to the same ethnic group as Christina, but they had never had any of the chances Christina had had. She felt compelled to help.

Of course, being an hour's drive west of her philandering ex-husband Kyle in the city that revered him as a football god was also a bonus to landing the job. Bella could see her father, and Christina could meet the court-imposed distance restriction.

She'd been in Morrisville two weeks now, and had used the time to rent a house, enroll Bella in school and get herself involved with some of Bella's classmates' parents, before starting work on Monday, November first.

When she'd been asked to help with the Brownie-troop function, she'd jumped at the chance. And had made an absolute mess of things.

She approached the fire truck, and caught an ongoing conversation.

"He's so hunky," one of the little girls was whispering to a friend as the fire ladder lifted skyward. "My mom's always wanting a new man. Says my daddy sleeps too much."

"Mr. Hunk," some other little girl agreed, latching on to the nickname.

With a smile to die for and a body to match, the man was compelling. Mr. Hunk. Christina could definitely agree with that assessment of the sexy firefighter.

Then again, Kyle had been a hunk, and look where that had landed her. Just because a man was as handsome as a prince didn't make him one. These days a woman was better off if she was selective. Thankfully, Bella hadn't overheard the girls' conversation regarding the fireman. Christina had no desire to explain what a hunk was.

"Come on, girls, let's do our crafts," Mrs. Sims called from the cafeteria doorway.

"Coming," Bella called.

"I'm going to go check the gym again," one of the firefighters said. He followed the girls back inside.

Christina turned to the firefighter who had spoken to her earlier. Mr. Hunk. Although the moniker fit, she really had to purge how attractive he was from her mind. Finding a new man was not a priority. Establishing her career and raising her daughter away from the glitz of Cincinnati was. "Thank you for your patience."

The firefighter shrugged, the high-wattage smile bestowed on the Brownies dimming fast. "It's all part of the job."

"Yes, but it isn't actually your job. You volunteer."

His blue eyes narrowed. "Exactly. I volunteer to do this job. We choose to do it because we help the community. This has been one of my easier calls."

"You're not disappointed when there's no fire?" Christina pressed, oddly finding herself wanting to understand what made a man like him tick.

His crossed his arms. "In a way I am. Once the adrenaline high wears off, though, believe me, we don't mind false alarms at all."

"But you dropped whatever you were doing, and on a Friday night."

"Yeah, well, that comes with the territory." He paused as one of his partners passed by with the big fan. "Seems like the place is all aired out. Duty calls to help load up. Excuse me."

Christina stood there for a moment. He deliberately ignored her presence and walked off, entering the school to retrieve the other equipment.

She laced her arms across her bare midriff and followed at a safe distance. Perhaps she was being too intense, too serious. She'd been so driven her whole life to prove herself—to her family, to Kyle. Perhaps she should just take things at face value. Maybe the firefighter meant exactly what he'd said. This was Morrisville, Indiana, and she was a fish learning to live in new waters.

And just because Mr. Hunk was the first man who'd aroused her interest in years—that meant nothing. Even if he found her appealing, she wasn't ready to date again.

She reentered the cafeteria, and within moments the last of the firefighters had left the school. Soon the fire truck pulled away, taking Mr. Hunk with it. Thank goodness she'd never see him again, Christina thought. She could bury the bad memory of this night forever.

BRUCE LANCASTER TOSSED his firefighter gear on the coatrack and hooked his black helmet over a peg. He stepped through the laundry room and into the kitchen of his small three-bedroom ranch. He'd dropped everything the moment the fire call had come through, and the TV still blared the ESPN sporting event he'd been watching. His plateful of chicken strips was gone, his dinner now in the stomach of the very sleepy and contented cat sleeping innocently near the heat register.

Bruce set the bag of just-purchased fast food on the kitchen table. Wise men with chicken-loving felines knew how to make stops at drive-through restaurants on their way home from firefighting gigs.

Bruce sighed and snagged a French fry, the rustling of the bag waking the cat. Boris, more interested in food than sleep, had come to investigate the smells and was sniffing the sack. Bruce finished one more fry and put the bag in the microwave for safekeeping. After every firefighting run he always wanted a shower before he ate, and tonight was no exception, even though the fire had been a false alarm. He was making his way to the bathroom when the phone rang. He glanced at the Caller ID and picked the phone up. "Hi, Granddad."

"Hi, Bruce. I didn't have a chance to touch base with you this afternoon. Welcome back. You ready for Monday morning's meeting?"

"Yes. I've got some files here at home and I'll be making final notations over the weekend."

"Great. I told your father not to take that three-month cruise with your mother. Not that I haven't always liked her, mind you, but this is a crucial time for the firm. We would never have hired some outsider as a full partner while I was at the helm, that's for sure, especially at the expense of a family member. You should have been named to that spot this year. Or two senior partnerships should have been offered. It's an insult that they weren't, and I'm in a mind to go talk to Reginald Morris again. He's certainly not like his father. No family values whatsoever. I'm sure your father knew nothing about it. If he did, I'd have to disinherit him. Just who is this upstart Chris Jones, anyway? Heard he went to Harvard. Probably an upper-crust New Englander who speaks six languages."

Tired, tonight Bruce didn't smile the way he normally did at one of his grandfather's legendary tirades. At seventy, Roy Lancaster had once argued a case successfully in front of the United States Supreme Court and received the majority opinion in his favor. Roy's father had founded the firm, but Roy had been the one to build Lancaster and Morris into the reputable and respected law firm it was today.

"I'm not certain who Chris Jones is," Bruce said slowly. He really didn't have any idea. "I've been in Indianapolis for the past four weeks, finishing up the Benedict appeal. Since I returned only two days ago, I still haven't met the guy. Heck, I've barely been in the office. The case requires someone who speaks Spanish, and I'm sure we'll get along fine."

"Always the politically correct one, aren't you? In my day everyone learned English," his grandfather scoffed. "None of this multicultural and bilingual fluff."

"And I'm sure our plaintiffs will learn English, as well. They are legal immigrants, Granddad. It just may take them a while. Their rights have been violated, English or none." Bruce raked a hand through his hair. He hated that his fire helmet made his hair stick to his head. "Can we talk later? I just got back from a fire call. I'm off to the shower."

"Ah, firefighting. How I miss it," his grandfather said wistfully, even though he hadn't fought a fire in at least forty-five years. "Was it a big one? I didn't hear anything on my police scanner."

"No, just a smoke machine that set off the alarms at the elementary school."

"Ah." His grandfather sounded disappointed for a second. "So, will I see you at the club this weekend?

Golf season's just about over. This is probably the last nice weekend we'll have. The grass gets really brown in November, and it becomes way too cold for golf."

"I'm not planning on playing."

His grandfather chuckled. "I see. A woman. Well, I'd better let you go."

"Yeah." Bruce let the fib stand and, after saying goodbye, dropped the cordless phone on his king-size bed. He'd been without a woman for a couple of months now, and celibate for longer than that. Maybe he was losing his touch, but the appeals case he'd just worked on had meant long hours and little free time to date. And he'd never been the one-night-stand type.

Now that the case was in the hands of the federal judges, Bruce hoped he'd have some leisure hours to scope out some new female companions. After all, the firm had hired Chris Jones as a full, senior partner. He could do the work.

Bruce backed into the hot shower spray and leaned forward so that the water cascaded over his neck and back. Who knew how much longer he'd be able to stay on Morrisville's volunteer force. While Bruce would have loved to be a paid firefighter on some department in a larger city, it wasn't what Lancaster boys did.

For multiple generations they'd been lawyers. Heck, one of his great-great-great-grandfathers had worked in Congress with Abraham Lincoln. The family accepted Bruce's volunteer firefighting only because the Morrisville citizenry considered it an honor, a duty and a matter of civic pride. The fact that Bruce's grandfather had once served in the fire department had also helped convince Bruce's worrying parents that a few more years wouldn't hurt. After losing one child at four months, his parents refused to lose another.

All in all, Bruce knew that he had a great life. At twenty-nine, he was well into his bachelorhood and enjoying it, much to the dismay of his parents. Morrisville girls married early, and the few women he'd met in Cincinnati didn't want to move more than an hour west to Podunkville, U.S.A. Heck, the closest Wal-Mart was twenty-seven miles away in Greensburg. Domino's Pizza didn't even deliver out here. Bruce liked it that way.

His thoughts drifted to the woman he'd seen at Morrisville Elementary. She wasn't local; his gut instincts told him that. And her ethnicity wasn't pure Caucasian. Was she Mexican? The water pounded on his back, and he turned and let it cascade over his chest for a moment before he reached for the soap. Not all Mexicans fit the dark-skinned, dark-haired stereotype.

The surrounding counties had been experiencing an influx of legal immigrants lately, especially those from Mexico. That was why the Title VII case Lancaster and Morris was representing was so important and why Bruce wanted to take it to trial so badly. Those workers deserved the same legal protections that native-born American citizens had. Just because the immigrant women didn't know the civil rights law didn't mean that companies like Morrisville Garment could circumvent it.

Winning this case would be a landmark, and he

could ride the wave of his success with it for a long time. He agreed it had been important to hire a partner who spoke Spanish and who could better communicate with the victims. He had taken French, which got him only as far as impressing a woman at Chez Jacques in Cincinnati.

But making this person a full partner? Admittedly, it stung Bruce that he hadn't been named senior partner this year the way everyone, including him, had expected.

Luckily, he'd been in Indianapolis at the time and had avoided the town gossip, which for a week had centered on his being passed over in favor of an outsider. However, winning this case, even under someone else's leadership, would seal his senior partnership.

Bruce tossed the soap back into the holder, reached for the shampoo and let his mind again remember the woman he'd seen at the elementary school. She'd seemed frazzled by the fire alarm. She'd been beautiful, though. Her brown eyes had been haunting, with a depth to them he hadn't seen too often before. He'd wanted to smile and reassure her, but had deliberately kept himself aloof and professional.

Unfortunately, she had a child, that cute little girl dressed up for the party as a black cat. A child made whoever the woman was off-limits, despite the absence of a wedding ring on her left hand. No, he liked his women young, single and dependent free. He wanted them to be able to pick up and go on a weekend trip at a moment's notice—which as a busy lawyer was often all he could afford. That meant no strings. No restrictions. No instant family. Although, when he did marry he wanted a lot of kids. He knew too well what being raised as an overprotected only child was all about. He rinsed his hair and turned off the water.

Besides, even if seeing her didn't break the parameters he'd set for himself, he was on call this weekend, plus he had to finish the case file so he could discuss it with Chris Jones Monday morning. He had other things to worry about than a woman with a child, no matter how beautiful or intriguing the woman was. Before he had to turn the water on again, this time to cold, he pushed her image from his mind and reached for the towel.

# *Chapter Two*

The insistent ringing Monday morning that invaded her dream of Antonio Banderas sweeping her away wasn't her alarm clock. Or her cell phone. It was her doorbell.

Christina sat straight up in bed and studied her bedroom. Something was wrong, and it wasn't the fading of her very pleasant dream. She blinked and attempted to focus. Except for the shrilling doorbell, the noises in the house were normal and the amount of light in her bedroom was the same as it always was at this time of the day.

Except that it wasn't this time of day. It was an hour earlier. She'd set the clocks back yesterday, after her mother had reminded her during their weekly Sunday-night chat that Daylight Savings Time had ended. The clocks were to "fall back."

The insistent noise at her front door still hadn't stopped, and Christina shifted. The clock read 6:30 a.m. Who would be here this early? Bella's carpool wasn't due for another hour. Christina drew on her robe and rushed through her house. She peered through the peephole, groaned and pulled the door open. "Marci?"

Marci Smith stepped back a pace and frowned. "Christina? Did you oversleep? Remember, I'm driving today. Is Bella ready?"

Christina's head pounded. "School's not for another hour."

Marci frowned. "What are you talking about? School starts in twenty minutes. Same time as every day. It's seven-thirty."

Christina's eyes widened. "It can't be. The clocks went back."

Marci's jaw dropped. She covered her mouth with her hand. "We don't set our clocks back. This is Indiana."

"Oh, my God." Houston, Boston, Cincinnati—everyone in the United States sets his or her clock back. Right? "You mean I'm an hour behind? I have a meeting at eight-thirty and I'm not even showered? And Bella!"

"You go get Bella. I'll wait here on the step. Megan's in the car, watching a DVD. As long as I can see her, she's fine."

"Bless you," Christina said. She turned on her heel and ran. Never had she moved so fast. She had Bella dressed, her teeth brushed and her hair combed in less than six minutes. Since Morrisville Elementary had a fantastic hot-breakfast program, Christina experienced some relief as she passed Bella over to Marci. At least Christina didn't have to worry about her daughter missing the most important meal of the day.

She herself would miss it, however. She didn't have

time for her normal bagel, black coffee and perusal of the *Wall Street Journal*. Instead, she rushed about, showering and shaving in under ten minutes and hopping on one foot as she wiggled into her pantyhose and shoes almost at the same time. She applied makeup in record time, as well.

Perhaps it was a good thing that Morrisville was such a small town. She made it to work only five minutes late. Her heels clacked on the marble tile as she entered the old brick building that had housed the law offices of Lancaster and Morris for more than sixty years.

"Christina Jones," she said when she reached the receptionist's desk in the middle of the cavernous lobby. "I have a meeting with Reginald Morris."

"Welcome, Ms. Jones. They're expecting you. They're already assembled in the grand conference room. Let me buzz them and tell them you've arrived."

That grand conference room had been the room in which she'd interviewed. It easily seated twenty, and no doubt all the senior partners were already there. Waiting for her?

She hoped not.

"Thank you," Christina said to the receptionist. The ornate three-story building, complete with a rotunda, was over one hundred years old. With high, arched ceilings and balconies, it had served as a county seat and courthouse before a new building had been erected in another town.

"Someone will be down in just a moment," the receptionist said. "Feel free to have a seat." She indicated a waiting area with old ornate chairs.

"I'm fine," Christina said. She clutched the Hermès briefcase that had been her gift to herself for landing the job. She hadn't been a shoo-in for the position. She'd competed against four other finalists.

Five minutes later, her feet beginning to throb from standing so long in her new two-inch Italian pumps, Christina turned as she sensed motion to her right.

"Ms. Jones." Reginald Morris, the fifty-something man with whom she'd done almost all her interviewing, approached, and she gave him a professional smile.

This job was the ticket to her and Bella's future. This job represented Christina's finally taking the reins of her own life and becoming the lawyer she'd always wanted to be.

Even though she'd passed the bar, it had been a while since she'd practiced law. She'd graduated Harvard Law School at age twenty-four, after intense years of full-time study. She'd racked up wins in a few impressive cases after law school, been promoted to full junior partner and called an up-and-coming, promising lawyer to watch. Then Kyle Jones had swept into her life and swept her off her feet. He'd insisted that she quit work and stay home once they were married.

She'd become pregnant with Bella, and not once had she regretted those years of "being home" with her child. But she was thirty-four now, and getting a late start. So if Lancaster and Morris had hired her only because they needed a Spanish-speaking female, fine. If they'd made her full partner only because it gave them much-needed diversity, so be it. This job had gotten her foot back in the proverbial door. Working meant being her own independent woman. It was a first step, and she'd take advantage of it. She didn't know where she'd go from here, but she knew it would be up.

"Mr. Morris. Good morning," she said.

He gripped her hand and then placed his left hand on top. "Christina, welcome. We are extremely delighted you're onboard. Your unique talents are going to win this case for our clients and for us. I have a premonition of great things ahead. Let me introduce you to all the senior partners."

"I apologize that I'm a few minutes late." Christina had learned that it was always better to be direct.

The corners of his eyes twinkled slightly. "Let me guess. You changed your clocks."

"Yes," she admitted.

He chuckled and patted her hand before he let it go. "Everyone who moves to Indiana makes that mistake the first year. Consider it a rite of passage or a bit of Hoosier State training. Of course, the legislature recently passed a law so that in 2006 the whole state will be on one time zone. Details to follow in April. We're this way."

"SO, ARE YOU READY to meet your new boss?"

"Lousy timing, Colin," Bruce said as his best friend peeled himself off the door frame and entered Bruce's office.

"When's the meeting?" Colin asked.

Bruce turned his attention back to the mound of papers on his desk. Even though his paralegal had faxed or couriered everything important to Indianapolis each day, the paperwork had multiplied while he'd been gone. "The big powwow started already. I'm not welcome until nine."

Colin winced. "Oh. That sucks. Even though you have to work with your new boss, you don't get to greet this person until later. Man, that's not fair. You should have been named a partner this year. Now me—I know I've got a way to go. I barely passed the bar, much to my father's disappointment. He claimed my grandfather was probably rolling in his grave."

"Bar scores are irrelevant. You passed. Besides, it's not like you had to worry about finding a job. You're a Morris and you were coming to work here."

"Exactly. And you're a fourth-generation Lancaster lawyer who scored the highest possible on the state bar that year and who has won some pretty impressive cases already. Your grandfather loves you. Your great-grandfather would if he were around. Heck, even my dad loves you, which is why I don't understand his decision. You should have been named full partner, also. To be passed over by someone outside just so the firm can claim diversity…well, I see it as an affront. And by a babe, too."

"Babe?" The word caught Bruce's attention. He put aside his legal brief and swiveled as Colin closed the office door. Bruce had to admit he hadn't really been listening. When Colin got on a roll, he could be as long-winded as Bruce's grandfather Roy. Bruce had learned to tune both men out.

"What do you mean, babe?" Bruce asked. "Some babe shot you down? You never lose out with women."

"Top of the bar exam, but still, as always, a lousy listener. You'd think as your best friend I'd be used to it by now. I even notice things like your shirts, which by the way your new tailor did a great job on. So tell me, how did we survive rooming together all those years in college? Anyway, I'm not talking about my women, though later I'll have to tell you about Gina."

Bruce arched his brow. "Gina?"

"Gina," Colin accented the capital letter *G* and made the shape of a woman's curves with his hands. "She even taught this dog some new tricks."

Bruce waved his own hand dismissively. He and Colin had always been confidants—sharing secrets and drowning sorrows when needed. "Okay, Gina later. If you weren't talking about her earlier, then who?"

"Oh, yeah, the new babe. Our new partner. Christina."

"Christina?" Bruce frowned as disquiet stole over him.

"Yeah, Christina Jones. Kyle Jones's ex-wife. You know, the Cincinnati Bengals' tight end?"

"She's our new partner? Chris Jones is a female?" Bruce's grandfather had had it all wrong. Bruce instantly knew that had been deliberate. Reginald Morris wasn't a fool.

"Boy, you have been out of the loop up in Indy, haven't you?" Colin checked to make sure no one could overhear him. "She's one hot mama, if you get my drift.

You know how I am with women. I've got to behave myself or I'll end up being part of that sexual harassment suit you both will be working on."

Colin attracted women like a magnet, but Bruce didn't care about that. Bruce had worked on cases with females before, and all had been totally professional. If his new boss were Miss America, it wouldn't matter.

But the fact that the senior partners had hired a female as full partner, instead of him, stung once again. However, he'd rise above this blow to his damaged male ego.

"You haven't heard a word I've said," Colin chastised.

"Uh, no," Bruce admitted. "I'm rather tired. I had a late call. Kitchen fire. A fry pan gone wild."

Colin rolled his eyes. Unlike Bruce, he'd avoided volunteering. "Lovely. How about we meet for a cocktail tonight at the country club. Say about five? I'll be over at the Ripley County Courthouse all day, doing closing arguments for the Watson case."

"That's fine. I'll call you if anything changes."

"Or if you need resuscitation after you see your new boss," Colin said. And with that he opened Bruce's office door. "Oh. Hey, Angela."

"Hey, Colin," Bruce's paralegal said as she stepped her very pregnant body by Colin and into Bruce's office. "Bruce, they just phoned. They'd like you in the conference room now."

Bruce glanced at his Rolex watch, a law-school graduation gift from his father. It was only eight-fifty. "Early."

"Maybe that's a good sign," Colin said with a nonchalant shrug.

"Maybe," Bruce said. He took one last sip of coffee, stood up and grabbed a breath mint. He popped the candy into his mouth and slipped into his suit jacket as the mint dissolved. "We'll see."

"I have to get the name of your tailor," Colin said, again eyeing the cut of Bruce's suit. "That is a great suit. Would work wonders on the ladies."

Bruce flicked a piece of lint off the subtle blue pin-stripe. "Salvatore Bandoria in Indianapolis. He and his wife are both seventy and all they do is make custom suits and dress shirts the old-fashioned way, as they did in Italy. They don't advertise. Remind me later to give you the phone number."

"I will," Colin said. "Good luck."

Those words brought back the reality of the situation, and Bruce shook his head as he walked past his paralegal and his best friend. "Thanks, but hopefully I won't require any."

"Yeah, right," Colin said with a wry grin. "You're off to that frying pan. You of all people should know firsthand exactly how much damage frying pans can do."

The fire late last night had scorched the entire wall of the kitchen, ruining the stove and several custom cabinets. But it wasn't as bad as it could have been. Deliberately not answering Colin, Bruce headed for the stairs. After all, how hard could a woman be?

"HE'S ON HIS WAY," Reginald Morris announced. He smiled at Christina. "More coffee before you jump in and get your feet wet?"

"Please," she said, and held out her cup. Unlike wine from Kyle, who had plied her with too much, coffee from Reginald Morris couldn't hurt.

Besides, by acknowledging the truth of why she'd been hired, she'd prepared for the worst.

There was one other female partner, Susan Jenkins. She handled trusts and estates, and at fifty-seven, she'd been with Lancaster and Morris for almost thirty years. Reginald Morris handled corporate law, as did three of the other senior partners, including Reginald's brother, Larry. There were ten senior partners total, including Christina, and all were present except for Roger Lancaster, who was on an extended trip with his wife and not expected until the week after New Year's.

Christina accepted another cup of java just as a movement at the door caught her attention. This must be Bruce Lancaster, descendant of one of the firm's founders. Everyone in the conference room had been raving about him all morning—he'd just done a fantastic job on an appellate case in Indianapolis, which was why she hadn't met him earlier.

"He'll be your right hand on this case," Reginald had told her. "He's the real reason the women brought their issue to us in the first place. His cleaning lady told him about her friends' plights, and he insisted they come talk to him, since their complaints were falling on deaf ears at their company. He's the one who, on their behalf, filed all the violations with the government. But he doesn't speak a word of Spanish."

Reginald's voice suddenly interrupted Christina's

retrospective. "Ah, here he is now, Christina. I'd like you to meet the man you'll be working closely with, Bruce Lancaster."

Christina automatically pushed her chair back and stood. The small crowd of people around him parted, letting him come into her field of view.

Her knees weakened and she gripped the edge of the mahogany table for support. "It's you," she said, unable to control her reaction as her stomach figuratively dropped to the soles of her Ferragamo shoes when Mr. Hunk, the firefighter who'd seen her at her worst, strode forward and stopped.

"You," he said, failing to mask the shock crossing his face.

Reginald's head turned as if he were watching a Ping-Pong match. He smiled uncertainly. "You two know each other?"

This was not the way to start her career return—first by being late and now by acting like a simpleton. "No," Christina replied.

"Yes," Bruce contradicted.

"I mean, we've met," Christina said, quickly covering. Damn the man!

"We have," Bruce said. He smiled widely, that charming Dennis Quaid grin of superiority, of one used to being master of his environment.

With the authority that only a member of a family could take, he patted Reginald once on the back, all while not letting his blue-eyed gaze lift from Christina's. "Reginald, Christina's an excellent choice for our firm. Just terrific. Angela's behind me with all the paperwork, so how about I bring her up to speed? Christina—may I call you Christina? Or did your résumé say Chris? That's the name I originally heard from my grandfather."

Christina planted her feet and struggled for mental balance. He had bulldozed her over. A jury would love him. Mr. Hunk was good, very good. "I prefer Christina."

He held out his hand, and she extended hers. He clasped it firmly, the amount of heat suddenly creating a most unwelcome shock.

"Christina, again let me welcome you to Lancaster and Morris. As I said, my paralegal, Angela, is carrying stacks of papers to the small conference room, which I've commandeered for our use for the entire length of the case."

"Great," Christina said. He released her hand, which allowed her equilibrium to normalize.

Reginald cleared his throat and took command of the room again. "Well, then, we'll let you two get to work. After all, time is money. Welcome aboard, Christina. I'm going to leave you in Bruce's excellent hands. He's one of the best lawyers we've got, and he'll show you all the ropes."

"Thank you," she replied. She had been thrown to the lions.

And then, one by one, all the partners filed out of the conference room, leaving Christina alone with Mr. Hunk.

Now all pleasantness was gone. Bruce Lancaster was the man whose partnership she'd taken.

And both of them knew it.

## Chapter Three

"Shall we?" he asked without preamble, demonstrating exactly who controlled the situation. With a wide sweep of his right arm, he gestured toward the double doors.

"Of course," Christina replied, her voice perfectly schooled into the tone her mother always irritatingly called "lawyerly neutral."

Christina grabbed her briefcase and clutched it to her side. This man would not affect her, and whatever fight he wanted to pick with her, she would not have it here, in the grand conference room, where anyone walking by could overhear them.

She stepped by him, taking little satisfaction that his nose wrinkled as her signature floral scent reached his nostrils. She paused just outside the doors, willing herself to remain poised and nonchalant. She had no idea where the small conference room was located.

"Need directions?" he drawled behind her.

She arched an eyebrow, and smirked. "You mean you know them?"

"Touché. Quick on her feet, with a bite to match the bark. Please, though, ladies first. The space we've been allocated is on the right, about three doors down."

Christina drew her shoulders up and strode down the hallway. Luckily, there weren't any curious faces to pass, and within seconds she'd entered the twenty-by-twenty-foot room. An early twenty-something woman whom Christina assumed to be Angela stood up. Her stomach protruded.

"Hi," Christina said. She held out her hand. "I'm Christina Jones. You must be Angela. Congratulations on expecting."

"Thank you."

"You'll be working with me on the case?" Christina asked.

"Only for the duration of it," Bruce told her smoothly. "I'm sure you'll have your own paralegal at some point. Make sure Reginald hires you one."

Making it very clear that although Christina may have taken his promotion, she wasn't getting his office staff, as well.

Angela's gaze darted between the two of them, as if she was trying to decide what the best course of action was. "I'll be here until Christmas, and then I'm on maternity leave for at least three months," she said. Her face broke into a wide smile. "She's my first."

"I have a little girl," Christina said, trying to find some common ground. "Bella's eight."

"Well," Bruce said with an obvious cough before Angela could answer, "that's all very nice, but we have work to do."

"I've got all your files stacked and your messages are right there. Do either of you need anything else?" Angela asked.

"No, thanks," Bruce said. "Just close the door behind you."

"Will do. Nice to meet you, Ms. Jones."

After Angela left, Christina faced Bruce.

"What?" he asked.

"You know, I'm surprised you didn't have her branded before she arrived. Tell you what, Bruce. Why don't you get all your anger off your chest early. Your paralegal, your partnership. Both now mine. Perhaps you should admit you're upset. If we clear the air, it might help us work together. After all, as you pointed out, we have a job to do."

"Do you have a degree in psychology, too?" He didn't wait for her to shake her head. "I didn't think so."

In a movement of control, Bruce sat down at the table. Christina remained standing. "Let's get a few things straight. I'm a Lancaster. I'm the founder's direct descendant. Roy Lancaster is my grandfather. Remember the Supreme Court case *Wedlock* v. *Storm*? He argued that one, and only one judge dissented. I descend from multiple generations of legal stock. I was top of my class and got the highest score on the bar that year. I could have worked anywhere."

She jutted her chin. "Your point is?"

The right corner of his mouth twitched. "Tell me, why should I be upset about waiting another year for a partnership? I'll be old and gray and this will still be my firm, my heritage. It will belong to my children, my sons and daughters. So don't try to use your pseudo-psychology on me. I'm not angry about the partnership. You couldn't be more wrong."

He paused for a few seconds, and Christina knew the litigator inside him wasn't finished. He'd only just begun.

And as much as she didn't relish the conflict, she found it slightly invigorating. She could already tell that he had a razor-sharp mind. He was quick on his feet, a man in control. He was self-assured, even when dealt a blow. She had to admit this man intrigued and stirred something inside her.

"Hmm," he finally said, "let's see how clever you really are and if we can do what you suggested and clear the air enough so that we can work together. How about you start by telling me what I have to work with. Since I was in Indianapolis, I missed your interview with Reginald. You only interviewed with him, correct?"

"Yes, once past the initial screening."

"That's what I thought. Your hiring went quickly. How many cases have you won lately?"

"That's on my résumé. I'm sure you could ask to see it. Or tomorrow I'll provide you a copy. I was a junior partner fast-tracked for a senior role at my last firm."

"So you feel you're qualified to work here?"

"Of course. There were other finalists and Reginald Morris thought I was the best. I did graduate Harvard top of my class. I did not just go there for an MRS degree." She paused only briefly. "I also have impeccable references."

He rolled his eyes. "Ah, stop avoiding the question. That's not what I asked. I asked how many cases you'd won lately. Do me a favor and be frank. I can at least respect honesty. Now you might understand why I'm truly upset. It's been eight years since you've last practiced. This is my case. I brought it in. I'm going to win it. While you might have had an impressive record years ago, your major qualification is that you speak Spanish."

"We—"

"Don't interrupt unless you have good reason to object. It's impolite and frowned on, especially in court. Let me simply sum up. You are here to be the female attorney the women can relate to, and to play interpreter. That's not any type of sexual harassment, either, just role definition and job description. You haven't had trial experience in years, and I'm not going to let you waltz in here and start over with a case as important and groundbreaking as this one. You're an outsider here, and that can be as grating as nails on a chalkboard."

"I'm—"

He ignored her interruption. "None of these women will know what Harvard is, much less know where it is. Most of them didn't even finish grade school. They won't wear designer shoes. They can't even afford the clothes that they make, even though they slave over each and every stitch. This is rural Indiana, not some big city. It's not an area that's culturally assimilated, or that has resources that celebrate ethnic heritage. You may be the same ethnicity as they are, but you are so far above them socially and economically that you might as well be one hundred percent white."

"Are you done?" Christina asked, her posture rigid.

"No, I'm not." Bruce swallowed, drawing his cheeks tight. "This is not playtime. It's not some genie costume, set off a smoke machine and everything will still be okay. Harassment is real for these women, and any misstep might cost us this case, and their futures, dearly. That I will not allow."

Christina froze her face into neutral and resisted the urge to clench her hands into fists and beat Bruce Lancaster into a pulp as she once had her cousin during a visit to Mexico City. She'd been ten. He'd pulled her pigtails.

Bruce Lancaster had done much worse. He'd insulted her integrity. He'd judged her incompetent based on a series of events beyond her control. He'd also belittled her—almost, but not quite, as much as Kyle.

Bruce was a jerk, probably just as bad as the ones they would be fighting. Mr. Hunk might be attractive, but he was not nice.

She took a deep breath and gave herself a much-needed continuance. She and Bruce would finish this conversation later, after she'd proved herself. Then she would rub his nose into every word he'd said. He deserved nothing less.

"Well," she managed calmly, her face a mask to hide her inner fury. "Now that you've finished venting in a misguided attempt to put me in my place, shall we actually begin to work on the case, or shall we continue to simply waste more valuable time?"

He stared at her, blue eyes wary, and she knew she'd caught him off guard.

"You see, Bruce—may I call you Bruce? I might not have a win record as long or impressive as yours, or even have close to your extensive courtroom experience, but that doesn't make me incompetent. I had an ex who spent years trying to prove that I was, and if *he* didn't succeed in convincing me, you won't, either. You've tried and convicted me based on circumstantial evidence and preconceived notions. Let me assure you, I won't fail."

"I don't have time for you to," he returned, his tone never losing its edge.

"And I won't." Christina leveled her brown eyes at him and held his gaze without blinking. Her body hummed with energy. "So why don't we do what we've been hired to do for these women, hmm? Shall you and I declare a much-needed truce, at least until you find some real evidence against me?"

He crossed his arms and studied her. His gaze traveled from her tight chignon, over the designer blue suit and down to her matching heels. "The jury's still out," he said flatly.

"Fair enough," she agreed. For now. Kyle had done enough damage over the years to her self-esteem. Bruce Lancaster had another thing coming if he thought she would simply roll over. She would never do that again, for anyone.

He gestured to a stack of brown expandable folders at one end of the table. "Those files contain the original interview notes. We've done no formal depositions at this time."

Bruce rose, moved a few steps and tapped a different stack of folders. She noticed his tightly clipped and filed nails—guy's nails that hadn't been professionally manicured.

"These files contain the violation reports that we've filed with the EEOC," Bruce continued. Christina knew the EEOC was the Equal Employment Opportunity Commission, the government agency in charge of overseeing all Title VII violations.

"Over there are the books I've pulled that have case history and applicable laws. Precedent is on our side, but with the recent changes in affirmative action legislation, there may be some chiseling at the sexual harassment laws, as well. Some of the women's cases are much stronger than others. We've already filed EEOC complaints on all of them, and submitted a demand letter to the company. If the company meets our demands, we'll settle. But if not, once the EEOC allows us to, we're filing in federal court for multiple violations of Title VII. Where do you want to start?"

"The beginning," Christina said, regaining some calm now that he was being reasonable. "That's usually the best place. Take me in chronological order."

"Okay." Bruce nodded and returned to his seat. She followed suit and sat herself opposite him.

They were still sitting there, engrossed in work, four

hours later when Angela knocked on the door and opened it. So caught up in the case, Christina hadn't even realized that the time had passed.

"I brought you both some lunch," Angela said.

"Thanks," Bruce replied easily, his demeanor relaxed, as if his working straight through the morning and lunch without a break was commonplace.

"I hope turkey sandwiches are okay," Angela said as she handed Bruce the deli bag.

"Perfect," Bruce said.

"They're fine," Christina agreed with a nod. Ever since she'd been pregnant with Bella, sliced turkey had held little appeal, mostly she ate vegan. But today she'd force herself to eat whatever sandwiches were in the bag. Her stomach growled. After all, it was after one.

Angela passed Christina the sack. "I bought two kinds of potato chips. Bruce likes sour cream and onion, but I got you plain, Ms. Jones."

"Christina," she corrected. "Plain chips are fine. Thank you for getting lunch."

Angela smiled. "Oh, it's no problem. I know how driven Bruce is. He wouldn't eat at all if I didn't force-feed him. Besides, I had an excuse to get a chicken salad sandwich from Kim's Deli. Ever since I've been pregnant, I've craved her chicken salad."

Angela paused. "So, do you require anything else? The small fridge on the floor over there is stocked with water and pop."

Christina wished she'd known that earlier. Her throat was parched, and some soda would do her good. Having been raised in Houston, where everyone called the fizzy beverage "soda," Christina still hadn't gotten used to calling it "pop" the way these Indiana Midwesterners did.

"I think we're fine," Bruce said. His expression dared Christina to contradict him.

"I'm good," she said. She pushed her chair back a little. "If you'd excuse me for a moment, though."

"The women's washroom is this way," Angela offered, as if reading Christina's mind. She held open the door, and Christina followed her out. Time to find more common ground and make some connection with Angela. If not, it would be long case.

"My feet are already tired. Is there a masseuse in there?"

"I wish," Angela said, taking the bait and talking. "I've gained two shoe sizes. My husband has the nightly chore of rubbing my feet. He hates it, but it's heaven for me."

"You're lucky to have a husband like that." Kyle hadn't done a thing except complain that when pregnant, she'd appeared as if she had a basketball wedged under her clothes.

"Oh, my Bryan is such a sweetheart," Angela confirmed. "We got married two years ago and it still seems like a honeymoon." Angela paused at the bathroom door. "You seem really nice, Christina. Don't let Bruce get you down. He's a slave driver, but that's only because he's so good at his job. He can't do anything less than one hundred and ten percent. It's not in his nature."

"Oh, don't worry. I'm fine," Christina insisted.

Angela bought the white lie, for she said, "Perfect.

He's a great boss. He really knows his stuff. Scored the highest on the bar, as I'm sure you've heard. And whatever you do, don't believe any of his so-called Casanova reputation. All made up by angry Morrisville women who can't land him. He's too married to his work. Anyway, call me if you have any more questions."

"I will," Christina said as she pushed the door open and stepped inside the women's washroom. After finishing her business and washing her hands, she took a long moment to study herself in the mirror. Tendrils of wheat-colored hair had come loose, and she pinned them back up. Her brown eyes were puffy, the result of her thinking she'd get an extra hour of sleep during "fall back." Thank goodness for Angela bringing food. When Christina had fled the house that morning, she hadn't given a thought to lunch. Tomorrow she'd pack one.

She headed back to the small conference room. Bruce was on the phone, the remains of his sandwich lying on the restaurant wrapper. Next to it sat a twenty-ounce bottle of cola, half-full.

"Go research the dissenting opinion on *Martin* v. *Blatt*. The judges locked two-one on it, and the uproar was so strong that the legislature went and voted in a law claiming that justice wasn't served. I think you'll find what you're wanting for your closing arguments there. The minute I hang up, I'll put Jessica on it and have her fax you the documents."

Bruce gestured toward Christina's unopened food as he listened to the caller. *Eat,* he mouthed before speaking into the phone again. "No, I wouldn't even open that can of worms. You don't want the jury off track from the main case. Always hammer your point, and reiterate that justice should be served." He paused. "Yeah. See you at five."

He hung up the phone and stared for a moment at Christina. "Get some pop."

He then pressed a button on the phone. "Jessica, Bruce. Dig up the dissenting opinion on *Martin* v. *Blatt* and get it over to Colin at Ripley, ASAP. Yeah. It's that important. No, I'm not going over there myself today. Just put a move on it. As if the deadline was yesterday. Colin is counting on you."

He ended the speakerphone call and raised his eyes to observe that Christina was still standing. "What? Do I have food on my face?"

"No."

"I work through lunch," Bruce offered as explanation. "Always have. It's more efficient than taking five minutes to go outside and stare at the birds. Too cold for that, anyway, now that the front moved through last night."

Christina walked over to the refrigerator and withdrew a 7-Up. Although she could use the caffeine, there was no Mountain Dew and she didn't like colas.

"That was Colin Morris," Bruce said, unexpectedly explaining the phone call. "You'll meet him at some point, I'm sure. He's a junior partner like me. He's also Reginald's son."

"He needed help on a case?"

"Surprises are never desired in closing arguments,

and the opposing counsel just landed a whopper. But Colin will rebound. He always does."

"And you just popped the answer right off the top of your head."

"Yeah." Bruce let the words, "I'm that good a lawyer" remain unspoken, but Christina heard them and was begrudgingly impressed. "I have a photographic memory and I'm good at trivia. One of these days I'd like to go on *Jeopardy.*"

"I don't watch much television." She didn't. Bella had discovered the cartoon channels. When she was married, Kyle had had a VHS-DVD-CD player and a plasma TV in every room. Christina had little use for more than one TV and a DVD player.

"So, where were we?" Bruce asked as she unscrewed the cap and put the soda bottle to her lips.

"I'd like a few minutes to eat in peace," Christina said. "Unlike you, I deliberately avoid working through lunch. That way I can have some time to clear my mind. I'd go find my office, but that would take too much time."

"They really did just throw you into the job feet first, didn't they? Fine. Eat." Bruce tapped his fingers on the table.

"Stop that," Christina said automatically, and unwrapped her sandwich. Bruce's fingers stilled.

"Thank you," Christina said. "That's better." She took off the top slice of sourdough bread. Sliced turkey, some white cheese that might be Swiss, tomatoes, lettuce, mayonnaise and black olives were underneath. Christina pulled some plastic tableware from the bag, removed the knife from the protective wrapper and began scraping the olives off the six-inch sandwich.

"That seems like a waste," Bruce observed, his lips puckering.

"I don't eat olives," she informed him simply. "Of any kind."

He shrugged. "Just make sure Angela knows what you like and she'll get it for you."

"I'll bring my lunch from now on," she said as she finished scraping.

"You have a food account," Bruce replied with a backward roll of his shoulders. "All the partners have an allowance, including the junior ones. It's there for times like today, or for when you entertain clients. Did they forget to tell you that, too?"

"It probably slipped my mind since I'm not entertaining at this moment," Christina said. Lovely. Now she probably appeared even more incompetent, making Bruce Lancaster feel even more superior. "I just prefer to bring my own food. I'll only be able to eat half of this."

She should remove the cheese, as well, but the cheese would drown out the flavor of the turkey. Pregnancy sure had changed her taste buds as well as her figure. She'd needed a nutritionist, a personal trainer and ten months of hard work to get back to her prepregnancy shape. By that time Kyle had had two road affairs, both with cocktail waitresses he'd picked up.

Christina had managed her weight with diet and exercise ever since, although now maintaining her weight was more of a healthy choice, and not anything that had to do with pleasing Kyle.

She returned the bread to the top of the sandwich and cut the sandwich into halves. She pushed one half aside. Then she saw Bruce's expression. "Are you still hungry? You can have the rest. Seriously."

"If you don't want it," he said. His arm snaked forward and he retrieved the sandwich. "Angela usually gets me a foot-long, but maybe today she was trying to keep everything the same."

Christina opened the bag of chips. It had been forever since she'd indulged and they were like forbidden fruit—too tempting. She'd only have a few. "She remembered your flavor of potato chips."

"To forget that is sacrilege," Bruce informed her as the conference room phone began to ring. He lifted the receiver. "Bruce Lancaster." His face darkened as he listened. "No, it's good you interrupted me. Tell her I'll be right there. She has to go in to work today. She cannot stay off the job. That will allow them to legitimately fire her. Tell her that she'll be safer today than ever before."

He put the phone down and stood, his portion of her sandwich remaining untouched. "We've got a crisis. Can you eat that on the way? Or I can buy you a hamburger on the way back? That is, if you're coming with me."

Her decision was instantaneous, even though she had no clue what he was talking about. "Of course I am." She rose to her feet. "What's happening?"

"One of our plaintiffs is refusing to go to work today.

She missed two days last week, and if she misses today without a doctor's excuse, the company will have legitimate reason to fire her."

"We're taking her to the doctor?" Christina asked.

Bruce was already halfway down the hall. "No. We're taking her to work."

## Chapter Four

Fifteen minutes later Christina understood what Bruce meant by her being an outsider. Not that it made his earlier comments about her competence less offensive or any less grating. He'd been right about one thing, though: this was a world she'd seen on TV, never in person. Even in Mexico City, her extended family lived behind walls in an affluent part of town, in luxury, with hired help. She had heard about those who lived in poverty and competed for handouts, but had never seen it for herself.

Here in Indiana, the words *ghetto* or *slum* didn't come close to describing the three single-story rundown motel buildings that sat crumbling next to a barren parking lot. Two rusted-out cars languished next to overflowing garbage Dumpsters. The parking lot was a crisscross of cracks filled with brown weeds. A rusted swing set moved slightly in the breeze, and the chain-link fence surrounding what had once been an in-ground pool had fallen in places. This place was a land that time forgot.

"Oh, my God," Christina whispered as Bruce's Ford 350 diesel pickup truck pulled up next to one of the buildings. Yellowed curtains that had decades ago probably been crisp white moved in several of the windows as the curious tenants peeked out, then scurried away.

"Put an interstate through and it's amazing what happens to places off the beaten path. This whole place ought to be condemned. But that's another lawsuit for another time. Earning just minimum wage, these people can only afford this lovely oasis."

"And they're all legal immigrants with work visas?" Christina asked, still not quite believing what she saw. The day was cloudy and overcast, giving the whole area a cheap, B-horror-movie feel.

"All the women in the lawsuit are legal immigrants. That was one law that the Morrisville Garment Company didn't violate. The migrant farm workers, who are mostly illegal, have already vanished for the season. This motel flourishes in the summer, with up to ten people in a room. No one but the churches pay much attention."

"It's a hellhole," Christina said, stepping her Italian shoes around a crusty pile of dog feces. A gust of dry wind sent dirt particles flying. Any grass had long browned.

"You'll learn to dress down except for court appearances. Professional, yet not flashy. The Average Joe does most of his clothes shopping at Wal-Mart in Greensburg."

"You're in a suit," she pointed out, seeking clarification. Her last employer, then Kyle, had always insisted she dress to the nines. Even her maternity wear had been expensive designer creations.

"Yeah, but only because I had that meeting with the partners. These people immediately think of the immigration service when they see people in suits."

Bruce walked up to one of the doors and knocked on the peeling paint. The number seven hung upside down by one nail and bounced erratically.

"María," he called. "María Gonzales. *Me llamo* Bruce Lancaster. Open the door. I must talk to you. Clara sent me."

The woman inside answered with rapid Spanish, but she still didn't open the door. Bruce knocked again. "¡María, *por favor!*"

"Let me try," Christina said. Already several doors had opened and heads had popped out, only to quickly disappear like in a Whack-a-Mole carnival game. "¡María! *Soy* Christina Jones, *la social de Bruce. Por favor abra la puerta. Le necesitamos hablar. Es muy importante.*"

"What did you say?" Bruce asked.

"I told her I'm your partner and I asked her to open the door. It's important."

"Oh." He appeared impressed, maybe stunned. But Christina had little time for satisfaction in her small victory as the worn door opened a crack and landed against the crash bar.

A woman peered out and launched a tirade in Spanish. Christina translated. "She says that the boss still tries to keep her on the line too long and that the ladies' toilets are broken and she cannot use the men's room in her area. He also leers at her and grabs his crotch."

"McAllister," Bruce said, knowing instantly whom María meant. "He's the worst. He's Donald Gray's nephew, which is probably the only reason no one's fired him yet. I'm going to phone OSHA about the broken fixtures."

"One more federal agency being involved can't hurt our case," Christina said. It was probably wise to call the Occupational Safety and Health Administration at this point.

"Rumor has it that they've been waiting for any excuse to get into the factory and snoop around for violations," Bruce said. "Maybe clogged toilets will do it. While I call, you must convince her that she has to go to work. She cannot give them a reason to fire her. Tell her that will let the bad guys get away with what they did. Say something. She must go to work today. She's already late."

"She said that she doesn't have time on her break to use the facilities in the other areas," Christina said. "She says she's getting a bladder infection."

"Oh, wonderful. Tell her the law provides even non-union factory employees with a bathroom break. If the toilets don't function in her area, she can use other ones without docked pay. We'll work out the correct federal agency for filing this new complaint later, but for today she must go in. You have to convince her. She doesn't even understand me."

Christina watched as Bruce pulled his cell phone out

of his pocket and punched a number. "Angela, get me the name and number of someone at OSHA," he said when she answered. "I want to know if it's legal to have nonfunctioning bathrooms on a factory floor. After that, report this to the EEOC, as well."

Christina stared through the small sliver of opened door. María Gonzales was a tiny woman, at most five-one. A roach crawled out from under a fallen leaf and scurried on the chipped concrete. Bruce crushed the bug with his foot.

Christina shuddered. She had a case to win and a job to do. No way would she ever be incompetent in front of Bruce Lancaster again, and it was time to prove herself. Besides, these women deserved much better than this hovel. They'd gotten through much already by being declared legal aliens. Just a little more time and their lives would be so much better.

"María," Christina began, *"tiene que ir al trabajo."* She saw the woman's brown eyes widen with fear at being told she had to go to work. Christina shoved her foot into the opening, wincing as her toes became pinched between the door and the wooden frame.

"No. You will not shut me out." Christina pushed her hand against the door to allow her foot some breathing room. The peeling paint stuck to her palm like children's stickers. Using rapid Spanish, Christina launched into an explanation about why María needed to go to work.

It took her five minutes of intense arguing, but finally Christina removed her foot and María Gonzales fully opened the door. Bruce was still on the phone and had moved a distance away.

María stepped out of the motel room, and Christina thought that maybe all the arguing with her mother had paid off. She'd used one of her mother's many emotional arguments almost verbatim on María. Before María closed the door, Christina could see an elderly lady and a small child inside. María's family. The reason she went to work, and the people Christina had convinced María that she couldn't let down.

"We'll drive you to the factory, and then I'm going to meet your boss," Christina said in Spanish. "Did you eat lunch?" Christina grimaced, knowing the answer the moment she asked the question. "We'll stop and get you something," she said.

Bruce flipped his phone closed and approached. María instantly lowered her head to her chest and gazed at her feet.

"Do not do that," Christina snapped at her in Spanish. María peered up in surprise. "Do not cower with him. You have heritage. You have pride." Christina nodded at Bruce. "We're ready to go. I told her we would take her to work, since everyone else on her shift has already left and they took one car. I also said we would get her some food for her break. I want to meet the company president."

"Donald Gray doesn't see people." Bruce said. "I've tried multiple times."

"Yes, but I haven't," Christina pointed out as they reached Bruce's truck.

Bruce considered for a moment. "Why not? It can't hurt."

Christina drew her suit jacket closer once they were under way. She'd opted for a silk shirt, and suddenly she felt exposed in her high-class wardrobe. No wonder María wore an Indianapolis Colts sweatshirt and faded blue jeans. The woman was working in a modern-day sweatshop.

After getting María some lunch, they drove to the factory in mere minutes, and Christina guessed that in the warmer months, many workers walked the distance.

How strange, Christina mused. She herself had gone to the finest schools in the United States and had never felt discrimination, but people like María Gonzales experienced it daily. People like María kept their deep-seated distrust of the government and struggled for the American dream, all the while attempting to assimilate into a culture they did not yet belong to or whose language they didn't even speak. And they had no idea that the law was on their side, providing them safe working conditions and the right to be treated fairly.

Christina had pointed out to María that the American government had issued her a green card when so many illegal immigrants went without. María had to go to work; it was up to her to create a better future for her family. The law would help. Christina had promised it would. And she was determined to keep the promise.

Bruce drove onto the grounds of the Morrisville Garment Company, giving Christina her first look at the buildings that were the scene of such injustices. They were nondescript structures, like so many other manufacturing facilities. Bruce stopped at a guard shack, signed in, and within moments, María had been seen safely to her employee entry door and had clocked in. María's immediate supervisor had been nowhere in sight, and Bruce parked the truck by the main entrance.

"May I help you?" An extremely bored receptionist turned her attention away from her fashion magazine. She was about eighteen, probably fresh out of high school last spring. She brightened when she saw Bruce's dazzling smile.

"I'd like to see Donald Gray."

"Do you have an appointment?" the girl asked, her expression hopeful.

Bruce shook his head and lifted the name plate. Julie, it read. "Not for today. Could you call him and tell him Bruce Lancaster's here?"

The girl shook her head and bit her lower lip. "I can't. He only sees people by appointment. I can take a message, though. You could leave a business card."

Christina watched as Bruce gave what had to be his signature smile. The man *could* outsmile Dennis Quaid. If Christina didn't know him so well, she'd be swayed, too. He had charm that could simply pull one into unprofessional thoughts.

Bruce pulled a card out of his pants pocket and toyed with it as if it were a poker chip. "Come on, Julie," he cajoled. "Call him for me."

"I shouldn't," she said, wavering a little under the deliberate high wattage.

"He'll be glad you did. Trust me." Those blue eyes twinkled, and Christina shifted her weight to the opposite leg, again acknowledging that Bruce Lancaster's charm affected her, as well.

As for Julie, she picked up the phone and dialed. "Yes, this is Julie in reception. Mr. Bruce Lancaster of Lancaster and Morris is here in the lobby and wishes to speak with Mr. Gray."

Her gaze darted back from Bruce to Christina. "There's some female with him." Julie lowered her voice. "She's wearing Prada. I recognize it from last month's *Cosmo*." She waited a moment. "I'll tell them." Julie replaced the receiver. "Mr. Gray is unfortunately indisposed, but his legal counsel, Elaine Gray, is on her way down."

"Thank you," Bruce said. He cupped Christina's elbow and moved her away from the reception desk. "It had to be your Prada. Elaine Gray never comes down, either."

"What—your charm can't sway her?"

Bruce grinned again. "Not since I went to prom with Marilee Becker, instead, no. She's thirty-two, went to Washington University, worked for a St. Louis firm and then returned home two years ago after a failed relationship."

"Out of curiosity, where did you go?"

Bruce turned slightly. "To Morrisville High School, like everyone else around here."

"No. I mean to law school. I just realized that not only do I not have any business cards yet, but I also have no idea about your background."

He leaned closer, and she stopped herself from stepping back. "I went to undergrad at Purdue and then Indiana University in Bloomington for my J.D. Yes, IU's public, but going there's a family tradition and it's one of the best law schools in the country. Ah, here she is. Smile, Christina. You're our ace. Make her worry."

Bruce extended his hand. "Elaine, how are you? You're looking exceedingly well. I'm sorry we just dropped in and I'm so glad you could take time out of your busy schedule to see us. Let me introduce you to Christina Jones, Lancaster and Morris's newest partner."

"Nice to meet you," Elaine Gray said politely as she and Christina sized each other up. Christina was five-nine, and Elaine probably five-ten. Bruce was taller than them both, but not by much.

Elaine's hair was platinum blond, almost white when compared with Christina's natural honey-wheat color. Up on the latest fashions from when she'd been Kyle's wife, Christina recognized a Dolce & Gabbana suit when she saw one, and that Elaine sported the latest haircut. Elaine extended her hand and gripped Christina's. When she let go, Christina resisted the urge to flex her fingers to revive them. "I take it you're new in town," Elaine said.

"Relocated from Cincinnati," Christina confirmed.

"Well, I hope you like it here. The shopping's terrible. I have to make quarterly trips to New York to find anything decent to wear. So tell me, what brings you both by? Our meeting regarding your little matter isn't until next week."

Christina kept her instinctive bristle hidden. Title

VII sexual harassment and ethnic discrimination were not "little matters."

Bruce, however, remained calm, as if he'd known exactly how Elaine would react and exactly how to play her. "One of our clients, María Gonzales, returned to work today. Her supervisor has been threatening to dock her pay if she leaves her work area. Unfortunately, because the women's facilities are inoperable, María must leave the area in order to carry out basic bodily functions. Elaine, my client should not have to fear going to work. Her supervisor cannot harass her for legitimate health and safety issues. On her behalf, I have contacted OSHA, and my paralegal will also keep our EEOC mediator abreast of this development."

"Since the worker's complaints did not come through proper channels or follow our company's reporting procedures, none of this has reached my attention," Elaine said simply. "I will of course investigate the matter immediately."

"Excellent," Bruce said. "I knew my clients and I could count on you to do the right thing."

Somehow managing to keep an unemotional and professional expression, Christina stared at Bruce. That was it? Elaine's answer had been more evasive than a fugitive on the run. "So you'll deal with it?" Christina couldn't help saying.

"We do take pride in our company," Elaine said. While her words were simple, the frosted tone was loud and clear. "Many of these matters lately are basic misunderstandings that are easily correctable if people would only follow the proper reporting procedures. We even use Spanish publications to educate our employees who speak English as their second language. Really, there is no reason for ambulance chasing at all. I hate seeing Lancaster and Morris lower itself to that."

"I'm glad you'll address it," Bruce said, ignoring the deliberate insult and instead reaching for Elaine's hand to shake it. "We've already taken up enough of your time. Ready, Christina?"

"Ready," Christina replied. She dutifully followed Bruce out to the truck, quite aware that Elaine watched them the entire time.

Once they'd climbed in and Bruce had driven out of the parking lot, Christina lashed out at him. "What were you thinking? You gave her time to fix any errors before the government shows!"

Bruce was unfazed by the outburst. "So what if Elaine gets the restroom fixed? That'll calm María down. Keeping María at work and getting all this changed is the big picture here. Donald Gray's one of those guys who thinks he's above the law. He cuts corners everywhere to make profits. He justifies his actions by saying at least he hasn't outsourced the work overseas. I'm sure that if they show, they'll find something."

Christina slumped against the leather seat back. "So why did we go see him?"

"Because your idea did have merit, even if the only result was to show you off," Bruce said wryly. "It tells them we're serious enough to hire a hotshot lawyer who wears Prada. Maybe they'll reconsider and settle, although I doubt it. Knowing the Grays the way I do, they're going to fight, and the EEOC is going to let us file."

"So you're creating smokescreens."

He nodded and grinned. "Exactly. I'm very good at what I do—you'll learn that. Speaking of good, you did a great job with María. Better than I ever could have done. Very impressive."

A compliment from the insufferable Bruce Lancaster. Christina turned toward him, but was met only by Bruce's chiseled profile as he kept his gaze firmly on the road. "Thank you," she said.

He didn't acknowledge her acceptance with a "You're welcome," but instead pressed on. "This little trip has cost us precious time completing what we were working on, so we'll review the rest of the papers when we get back and formulate a plan of attack. We'll probably work until at least seven or eight tonight. We can order dinner using those food accounts I mentioned earlier."

"I can't," Christina answered simply.

This time Bruce did turn toward her. "What do you mean you can't?" He glared.

"Bella's after-school care closes at six. I can stay until five-thirty at the latest every night. That's it. When I was hired, I made that perfectly clear, and Reginald Morris agreed. Besides, don't you have to play fireman?"

"I'm not on call tonight," he said tightly.

"Well, I am. Except when Bella is in school, I have a motherhood role 24/7. And, unlike the factory workers we're representing, I know exactly what is required of me on the job. Working past five-thirty isn't."

"Such commitment," Bruce said. He was obviously irritated. "We have a timetable, Christina. Many of our clients work second or third shifts. They don't fit your hours."

"I will see what I can arrange when it's absolutely necessary," she said, refusing to concede. "But let's get some things clear. Don't you ever dare question my commitment. I am committed to my daughter, my family and my job. I will work my tail off for Lancaster and Morris. I can't do any less. Don't battle me, Bruce. I've had my boxing gloves on for most of my life. I had to fight to convince my mother about my going to Harvard and later about divorcing Kyle. Both experiences taught me to fight first and ask questions later. I doubt that would do either of us any good."

Silence descended as Bruce drove back into the parking lot and Christina studied her Cartier watch, a very expensive guilt gift from Kyle when she'd first become suspicious of his extramarital activities. How had it become after three-thirty already? The afternoon had flown by. Highly aware of Bruce's rigidity and the fact that he'd glanced at her every few seconds during the drive, she climbed out of the truck the moment he killed the engine.

"Christina, wait," Bruce called after her.

But as a blast of cold November air blew by, Christina refused to turn around. Instead, she strode for the entry doors. Damn Bruce Lancaster. The man was infuriating! One minute she respected his legal mind; the next minute she wanted to throttle him. They could at least continue this argument inside, where it was warm.

REGINALD MORRIS TURNED AWAY from his executive office window. He'd just spent the afternoon in an unexpected meeting with Roy Lancaster. The old coot had arrived in full regalia—double-breasted business suit—wanting to meet Christina himself. A firm believer in the two-martini lunch, he'd probably had one too many cocktails at the Morrisville Country Club.

The trouble with Roy was that, even though he'd retired long ago, he still considered the company his baby. Hell, the old boy had even indicated in his will that he wanted to be laid out in state in the middle of the rotunda as if he were some president. All of Morrisville, of course, would expect nothing less and would make their appearances and trundle by. Unfortunately, Roy Lancaster was as sharp as a tack, alcohol or none. And Roy had not been very thrilled to hear about his grandson being passed over for a partnership. He'd been more offended once he'd realized that Chris was actually a Christina. No wonder Roy's son had escaped on a world cruise with his wife while the deed was done. While Reginald missed his own deceased father dearly, in a way it was good that he wasn't around to gang up with Roy. One former senior partner haunting the place was more than enough.

Reginald exhaled his pent-up frustration. The partners had agreed that it was time to diversify. With the growing Hispanic population in the region, the ancient firm of Lancaster and Morris needed to evolve if it didn't want to become a dinosaur. Thus, they'd hired

Christina. She'd been the best candidate, and the one most determined to succeed. Reginald had seen true motivation in Christina to excel, to prove herself. She was hungry. And that was what he wanted. Someone who sought a career with Lancaster and Morris, not just a job.

He watched from the window as she stormed across the parking lot, Bruce Lancaster storming after her. Reginald winced slightly. He'd known Bruce would be angry at being passed over for a promotion, but the partners had made it clear that next year was Bruce's year. No matter what.

Unless, perhaps, his case bombed.

And from the way Bruce's new superior was outdistancing him, things didn't seem to have gotten off to a good start.

Reginald stepped away from the window, went to his desk and pressed the intercom button on his phone. "Send me Bruce once he gets in."

"Yes, sir," his secretary said.

Reginald nodded to himself. He hadn't had a chance for a one-on-one with Bruce since his return from Indianapolis. Well, he'd known Bruce since birth, had treated him practically like his own son. Bruce just needed to be set straight. He was a sharp boy and a good one. Yes, Bruce should see the light and error of his ways.

And Reginald considered himself just the man to help.

# Chapter Five

As Bruce strode across the parking lot, irony slapped him in the face along with the wind. He couldn't believe he'd forgotten that he'd promised to meet Colin at the country club lounge at five. The cold wind picked up, and Bruce winced as the bitter breeze tried to sneak under his suit coat. He'd been a royal ass with Christina about working late, for nothing.

Why she got under his skin so much he didn't have a clue, but the woman grated on his nerves. He'd reacted without thinking, which was something he never did. He'd lost control, another something that never happened. He certainly couldn't be attracted to her—okay, maybe a little, especially when he thought of that genie costume—but she was off-limits because he refused to fraternize with any female from work. No matter how great she'd looked from behind as she stormed into the law firm.

Not that any of that mattered, or that he had realized how wrong he was. Ms. "Boxing Gloves" had no intention of letting him back into the ring for another round to straighten the matter out.

Damn, Bruce mentally cursed. Things in Indianapolis had gone so well, and he'd had such high hopes for his return to Morrisville and this case. Work was pure adrenaline—and Bruce thrived on it. He loved piecing together the argument, was thrilled when the jury or judge returned the verdict Bruce wanted.

Driven to prove himself and his place in his impressive lineage, not once had Bruce missed settling down. He didn't understand single women with kids, and because of that, his perfect job had just turned into a nightmare. The holidays were coming, and they weren't going to be very merry unless he and Christina Jones could work things out.

A prickle of awareness wiggled up Bruce's spine and he lifted his gaze. Reginald Morris was staring out a second-story window, an obvious frown on his worried face.

Bruce gave a wave, but wasn't surprised when it wasn't returned. There were two coveted offices in the ancient building, at opposite ends. The Morris family office had a northern view of the parking lot and Main Street. Bruce would eventually inherit his father's office, with its quieter southern view of the city park.

He actually preferred that one.

"Mr. Lancaster," the receptionist said as he entered the building without slowing his step, "Mr. Morris's secretary called down. He wishes to see you."

And without her speaking the words, Bruce knew the summons meant immediately. "Lovely," Bruce said to himself, avoiding the profane cuss word he'd rather have uttered. He saw the elevator door close, effectively hiding Christina's face from view.

One thing about old brick buildings—the elevators moved at a snail's pace. Bruce took the grand stairs two at a time and caught Christina as the elevator door opened.

"We need to talk," he said, stopping her exit.

Her shoulders tensed and her expression turned haughty. "Right now I'm going to try to find my office. I have nothing further to say to you."

He gestured to the ceiling. "It's probably on the third floor. There'd be no space on the second unless they tossed someone. That I don't think happened in the months while I was gone."

"I'll find out by myself," Christina said, savagely punching the button that would shut the elevator door.

Bruce blocked the closing door with his shoulder. He winced for a brief second before the door retracted. "I'll come up when I'm finished. Reginald Morris asked to see me."

"Why?" A flicker of interest crossed her face and Bruce wondered if she hoped he was getting fired. Like there was a fat chance of that.

"I have no idea, but I'm guessing it's something about the case."

She frowned. "Then why didn't he call for me?"

"Who knows. I haven't had much of a chance to meet with him since I got back. But if it is about the case, I promise to tell you once I find out."

"I'm leaving at five-thirty."

Bruce's watch showed that it was nearing four. "I meant to tell you about that."

"Bruce." Reginald Morris's secretary's voice came clearly down the hall. "He's waiting."

Bruce stepped back and faced the secretary. "Tell him I'm on my way." When Bruce pivoted again, the elevator door had already slid shut and Christina was gone. He walked down the hall and rapped on Reginald's office door.

"Bruce, ah, there you are. Come in." Reginald Morris waved magnanimously from the middle of his office. "Busy day?"

"Very," Bruce replied.

Reginald gestured to the burgundy leather wing chairs that stood in front of his oversize mahogany executive desk. "Have a seat. Take a load off. I heard that you were in the field today."

"We were. We went to make certain that María Gonzales went to work today. The factory is having some restroom issues. Rumor has it that OSHA's on its way."

"Ah, the feds. I'm sure they'll find at least one violation to cite to make the hour's drive worth their while. So Christina went with you?"

Bruce tensed. Having grown up around Reginald Morris, Bruce knew exactly when the man had something up his sleeve. Like now. "She went with me."

"Did something happen? She appeared to be in quite a hurry as she crossed the parking lot."

"It's cold out there. Besides, she was excited to find her office," Bruce said, the half-truth sliding smoothly off his tongue. "I don't believe any of you have ever shown it to her. She doesn't even have any business cards." Bruce let his voice trail off, and was rewarded when Reginald squirmed slightly.

"No, I suppose we did overlook some details in our rush to get her started immediately. Coming into the middle of a case is always so hard. Which, my boy…"

Reginald paused for effect and Bruce hid his distaste. Although he'd practically grown up at the Morris house, he still hated when Reginald called him "my boy." Bruce was a man. Hadn't he proved that with all the cases he'd won?

"Yes?" Bruce replied, as required.

"Son, you go easy on that girl. She's new. I know her coming in as partner over your head is hard for you, but the choice was a necessary one. In this electronic age people don't have to use their local lawyer anymore. They can use one of the big-city boys, those slick up-starts who have no sense of tradition and are only out for big bucks and billable hours. You understand tradition."

"I do," Bruce said. His life was proof of that.

"That's why, when we did this, we knew that if anyone would understand, it would be you."

"You should have given me a heads-up."

Reginald nodded. "We should have, but quite frankly, we didn't want to tip our hand too early, and by the time she was hired, it was too late. You were on your way home from Indianapolis. We had to be secretive. Your grandfather's been breathing down my neck all day."

Reginald turned away for a moment and gazed out

the window before facing Bruce again. "I'm sorry for keeping you out of the loop. But what's done is done. And right now, I need you to be onboard one hundred percent, even though you don't like the situation. Put yourself in Christina's position. You know all about dreams and modifying them to fit certain expectations. Imagine what's she's been through, coming to Morrisville after the high life in Cincinnati that she had. Rather the opposite of what usually occurs. Our young folk take off. You would have."

Reginald had him there, Bruce realized. Bruce would have loved to be a firefighter somewhere. But he was a Lancaster. The older man continued.

"Bruce, I'd like her to stay. There's a whole population out there we can reach with her repertoire, and I want to reach them. I want you to help us out, son. Be kind to Christina. Although your anger at the partners is justified, put it aside and work with her."

He couldn't stop himself. "She hasn't practiced in eight years!"

"Yes, but her credentials are solid and she's sharp. So mentor her. Your legal skills combined with hers, and her knowledge of the Mexican culture, will allow us to take this company in the direction it needs to go in order to build a positive future. You gave up firefighting in a big city so you could commit yourself to this firm. Your father and I are counting on you, Bruce."

Reginald's office, that deep mix of burgundies, mahoganies and woodland greens, subtly reinforced the idea of tradition. Bruce exhaled. "I know you are."

"No, I mean we're really counting on you. Your grandfather's traditional and old-fashioned. He needs a hobby. That aside, you, though, are the future of this company. You're a brilliant lawyer and I'd like you to work personally with Christina. Teach her the ropes. As I said, she's a smart one, that lady, and she'll catch on quick. In addition, be her friend, if you will, a male compatriot she can rely on. She has no one. Show her and her daughter the town. Introduce her to Morrisville society. Go above and beyond, Bruce, within reason."

Within reason—a euphemism for remain purely platonic. Don't look, much less touch. Bruce sat there. As if he'd touch Christina with a ten-foot fire pole. And even if he wanted to—that idea suddenly lurked like a devil on his shoulder—he doubted Ms. Boxing Gloves would let him within two inches of her person before clobbering him.

"Okay, I can do that," he said slowly, as though testing the waters to see if Reginald had finished his spiel.

The old man smiled once, pleased with Bruce's answer. Then he sobered. "Great. I'm glad we've had this little conversation. When you see my grandson at the club tonight, please refrain from mentioning it. Colin shouldn't be privy to everything that goes on around here."

Speaking of meeting Colin, did Reginald Morris have spies everywhere, or was Bruce's life just that predictable? He took the cue and stood. "Of course I won't mention it. I can be the soul of discretion."

"That's one of your most admirable traits. Now, why

don't you go on up to Christina's office and make peace? Let's end her first day on a positive note."

The "Yes, sir" wasn't necessary, and Bruce left the office without another word. Reginald's secretary gave Bruce a sympathetic smile as he strode by. He then took the steps to the third floor two at a time.

UNTIL THE MINUTE Bruce Lancaster stepped through the door, Christina had been thinking that her office wasn't all that terrible. She was upstairs, on the opposite side of the building from Reginald Morris's office. The ten-by-ten room had two windows that, when the blinds were open, provided a bird's-eye view of the park.

She wasn't sure what the room had been previously, but it was obvious that they'd tried to make the place welcoming. The walls had been freshly painted a neutral beige and new carpet had been installed. She had new oak furnishings: a desk, two tall bookcases, a computer hutch and credenza and two matching file cabinets. In an attempt to make the walls less bare, they'd hung two prints of some pastel artists Christina didn't recognize. The room desperately needed homey touches—her daughter's artwork, plants, family photos, even those beanie baby stuffed toys people stuck on their cubicle shelves.

"Busy?" the man who'd begun to annoy her more than her ex-husband asked.

Too busy for Bruce? Always. "No," Christina replied, her better judgment to be civil winning. "What is it now?"

"Actually, I wanted to see if we could start over. You know, not let the sun go down on this day without finding a way to coexist."

She stared at him, her disbelief clear. "And you think that's really possible?"

He gave her that charming smile she was trying hard to hate. That smile did things to her—for instance, disarm her despite her desire not to be swayed. "Well, yeah, Christina, I think we can. We're both adults and professional. Surely we can put this pettiness behind us."

She refused to give in easily. "I didn't realize I had an issue with pettiness. Seems to me you're the one with the proverbial chip on his shoulder today."

"Probably," Bruce admitted, the left corner of that cheeky mouth inching guiltily upward. "If it helps, I apologize. I was in Indianapolis when you were hired, so yes, I doubt I've taken much well. And I'm used to being the lead on all my cases and doing things my own way."

"Doesn't share well with others," Christina quipped as she covered her shock with a joke. He'd apologized?

"Exactly." Bruce raised his hands in a gesture of surrender. "I'm here to raise the white flag."

"Which means Reginald Morris chewed your butt." Christina searched for the truth behind Bruce's sudden change.

"That, too," Bruce admitted with a guilty laugh. "But as I'm family, and I practically lived at his house growing up, I know his bark's worse than his bite. He was probably more irritated that my grandfather came down and haunted the place today."

"I didn't think your grandfather was dead."

"He's not."

"Oh." Christina contemplated that for a moment. The sincerity she was observing in Bruce was genuine, not something contrived for her benefit. "I take it your grandfather can be a thorn."

"When he gets a notion something's wrong, it's as if he's never retired. Since my father's on vacation, Reginald got the full brunt of my grandfather's visit."

"Ah," Christina said. "I see."

"You'll have an even better picture once you finally meet Roy. Trust me, he'll be by at some point to scope you out personally and grill you unmercifully."

"That sounds delightful," Christina said with a shake of her head. "I'm starting to wonder if I've entered the twilight zone. I wanted to take the job in L.A. Unfortunately, my divorce decree limits my travel range to seventy-five miles from Cincinnati."

"I'm sorry," Bruce said.

"Are you really?" Christina arched an eyebrow. "Or are you just another person saying the right thing and wondering just why Kyle Jones's ex-wife needs to dirty her hands and work for a living?"

"I'd be lying if I didn't admit that the thought hadn't crossed my mind at some point," Bruce replied honestly. "But it's none of my business. What is my business is that I treated you poorly today, and I have no excuse."

She rested her chin on her left thumb and forefinger and studied him. Could he be different from other men?

Trust came so slowly for her. She straightened. "No double speak or lawyer talk. That's a refreshing change coming from you. Well, let me assuage your curiosity. I always wanted to be a lawyer. Help the less fortunate, give back to the community, et cetera. Unfortunately, a man with more brawn than brains and more libido than integrity sidetracked me along the way.

"I *could* sit on my pretty Prada-clad rear end and collect my support checks. But that would make me just as bad as those society fluffs you read about. That's not me. I can't sit idly by and do nothing, especially when there are women like María Gonzales in the world who deserve so much better. So, I choose to work, just so I can help people like her. I am going to be someone and something besides Kyle Jones's bimbo. I was that long enough."

"And I respect that," Bruce said.

His answer surprised her, and she leaned back in her chair. An undercurrent of an undisclosed nature buzzed in the room. "Do you really?"

"Actually, yes. I wanted to be something besides just another lawyer in a long line of Lancasters who have been nothing but. I wanted to be a firefighter. But duty to my family said otherwise. I can play at firefighting, but I can't move to a big city and become a full-time member of a force. I know exactly what giving up a dream means. It means you start over and learn to be satisfied with what you have."

"Yes," Christina said, impressed that he'd actually understood. Perhaps Bruce Lancaster did deserve another chance. "That's what it means."

"So have dinner with me tonight."

"What?" Surely she hadn't heard him correctly. That would go against everything that they'd just settled and….

"Dinner. Oh." Understanding dawned on his face as he comprehended her expression. "Not like that. As law partners. Why don't you have dinner with me. Let's continue this conversation somewhere on neutral territory, away from the office."

"I have to pick Bella up from child care."

Bruce made his decision instantly. "Bring Bella along. Christina, this job is going to become 24/7 whether you like it or not. Bella might as well meet me, since I'll probably be bringing work over on the weekends, especially once the case gets closer to trial. And everyone, including the Grays and the EEOC, knows a trial is inevitable."

He was correct, of course, and Bruce had been so good with the girls at the elementary school. Yet she hated her predicament. Still, following a dream was about sacrifice. She wanted to be successful in her own right. She didn't plan to live in anyone else's shadow ever again. Being Bella's mom was a noble calling in itself, but Christina still found herself driven to have more. If other women could blend career and family, she could, too. She wanted it all.

"So, dinner? You, me and Bella?" he repeated.

She had to find out. "Is this one of Reginald's orders? Be kind to the strays?"

"Yeah, perhaps he suggested it. But let me tell you, I don't do anything that I don't want to do."

From Bruce's forceful tone and the determined set of his jaw, she knew those words were pure truth, with no ulterior motives. "Okay," she conceded. "Dinner. But we have to be home early. It's a school night and Bella's always in bed by nine."

"Good." He seemed pleased. But he might not be as agreeable after she made her next demand.

"May I suggest a restaurant?" she asked.

He shrugged. "Sure."

"McDonald's PlayPlace?"

Bruce squinted. "What? I was thinking more like the club. That way you could also meet some of Morrisville's citizens."

Christina shook her head. "I'm going to veto that. Bella's attention span will last all of ten minutes, and that's only if the club provides crayons and picture menus with puzzles and games."

"Ah," Bruce said. He sighed and gave an exaggerated shrug. "Not even enough time to order appetizers."

"Exactly. Bella's cute, but I'm nothing except realistic. Struggling with a squirmy child is not how I'd like Morrisville society to remember me. She's had it rough enough as it is being uprooted. Maybe next time."

"McDonald's it is." Bruce grinned and Christina felt the warmth of his smile. She laced her fingers together underneath her chin.

"Great. We've successfully negotiated our first compromise. How about I meet you there at six?"

"You'll have enough time?" he asked.

"It's five minutes from the elementary school."

"Six is fine," he answered with a nod.

"I'll see you there, then," she said, and that was that.

But after Bruce left, Christina stared at the beige walls. What had she been thinking? She'd agreed to go to dinner with Bruce Lancaster, resident shark. Not that she found Mr. Hunk interesting. Well, perhaps she did just a little. Honestly, maybe a lot. His legal savvy was off the charts, and she had to admit that she could probably learn great things from working alongside him. She'd studied with some of the top minds at Harvard, but Bruce was a real in-the-trenches type of guy who rolled up his sleeves and got to work. He didn't mind getting dirty, or doing whatever it took to make people's lives better. Despite their tenuous start this morning, he had a few qualities that awed her.

He'd grown up pretty pampered, she could tell, with his future in Morrisville mapped out for him since birth. Her future had been turned upside down several times.

She didn't even know how long she planned on staying in Morrisville. Was the place just a stepping-stone, or was it where she'd find all her needs met forever and ever? Not having any idea, she'd rented the cute bungalow, not purchased it.

Morrisville itself had been a culture shock after Cincinnati. The town's local supermarket doubled as a deli, and the entire building would have fit in Kyle's four-car garage. While the store proudly boasted that it had everything, it only had one variety of everything, unless you counted beer and soda. Then you had two brands of each: Miller and Budweiser, Pepsi and Coke.

Christina had discovered that organic foods grown locally were available by the dozen, when in season. The many roadside stands, now closed for the winter, attested to that. But ethnic varieties and specialties, even gourmet sauces and bread choices besides basic white, didn't exist without a minimum of a half-hour drive.

Christina sighed. Morrisville had seemed the perfect place to reinvent herself, to discover exactly who Christina Miranda Elise Sanchez Jones was and where she wanted to go from here. She hadn't wanted to go back to Houston, another large city where she could be swept away, lost in the crowd. Once home, her family would have pitied her as a failure, a woman who hadn't been able to keep her non-Hispanic man from wandering.

No one in her gene pool had ever suffered Christina's fate. All her cousins and her two siblings had successful marriages and at least two children. Christina was the middle child, and she'd broken her family's cultural mold by marrying Kyle. Her mother had railed against it, but Christina had been under the haze of starry-eyed love. Hindsight let her see straight.

Divorced people, Christina had found out these past ten months, didn't fit in anywhere. Married women were afraid you might try to hit on their husbands, and shielded them as if you'd grown two horns and had a contagious disease. Many of Christina's so-called former friends had simply turned their backs: no odd numbers allowed.

As for the men: oh, they hit on you, and the adage that the good ones were all taken or gay was true. The most inappropriate men came on to Christina, not for who she was but for what she had. They saw a free ride, a woman with money; a way to sit on their duffs and lie on the couch and do nothing. After the first one-date test case, she'd refused to date again, and had resolved that should she ever date again, no man would get close to Bella until Christina knew the relationship was serious. Bella had already suffered the misfortune of becoming attached to some of the women who hadn't realized they were just one of Kyle's revolving-door relationships.

When Christina had decided to leave Kyle a year and a half ago, the decision had been emotionally wrought and nightmarish. He'd been more concerned with his precious image and had kept asking how she dared to tarnish it.

The legal mess had been ugly. Their divorce had made *Entertainment Tonight* and even been a joke or two on *The Tonight Show*. Ten months later, her divorce had been final, and eight months after that she'd been in Morrisville, having not wanted to spend another moment in Cincinnati. Even her new neighborhood had not been pleasant. One former neighbor had suggested that she'd tarnished the block and that perhaps Christina should find a new residence where more single people lived. So, while the city might be wonderful, there were too many ghosts and people who now turned their backs.

Christina Jones, replaced by a younger arm ornament and discarded with a hefty settlement and monthly child support, had become yesterday's news and a has-been. Morrisville was a clean slate, untainted and unbiased. Here she could mold herself, not have someone mold her. She just hoped she didn't somehow mess up her life yet again by making a choice that didn't work out. That was her greatest fear.

And letting Bruce Lancaster under her skin in any context spelled danger. She had to admit she found him fascinating and that made him dangerous. He could upset all she'd worked so hard at accomplishing, and with one disarming grin topple everything she was trying to build. But she could use a friend, and wondered if that was possible.

"Still here?" Reginald Morris rapped on the door.

"I'm just about to leave," she said. "I have to get Bella by six."

He stepped into the room. "I just wanted to reiterate my welcome and congratulate you on surviving your first day. Hopefully, it wasn't too hectic."

Christina pushed a loose strand of hair behind her ear. "Thanks. It wasn't too bad."

"Good. I know we've forgotten some things—this office is pretty bare. You probably don't even have a stapler. Make a list of everything you'd like and give it to my secretary tomorrow afternoon. She'll order it all. Your computer will be up and running tomorrow, as well. I do want to apologize for our disorganization. We were just so excited to have you onboard that we let a bunch of little things slide. We should have been better prepared. Bruce reminded me that we even forgot your business cards. The printer will have those delivered tomorrow."

"I'm glad to finally be here," Christina said.

"So are we. Now, run along. Go get your daughter a bit early. I'm sure she's wanting to see you."

Christina rose. "Probably. Thank you."

"It's nothing." He suddenly grinned. "Just remember to reset your clocks when you get home. You're an Indiana resident now." With a gentle chuckle that indicated more amusement than censure, Reginald disappeared back down the hall. Christina grabbed her coat off the coat rack. Five-fifteen. Plenty of time for some mother-daughter time at home before meeting Bruce for dinner.

"SO HOW'D IT GO TODAY? She's hot, isn't she? A real looker."

Bruce sighed and stared at his scotch. He swirled the amber liquid around in the cut-glass tumbler. Perhaps meeting Colin in the country club lounge hadn't been such a good idea after all.

"I thought you wanted to discuss the case," Bruce said. "Or that girl? What was her name?"

"The judge declared court recessed until tomorrow. Not much to tell. This isn't something the jury's being sequestered for, so they'll more than likely have a verdict by lunch. As for the girl, you mean our hot new senior partner, yeah?"

Bruce bristled, finding Colin's cavalier bachelor attitude annoying, especially in the context of Christina. "No, I didn't mean Christina Jones at all. You mentioned…" Bruce racked his brain. Erica? Ellen? He drew a blank. "That girl. You know. The old-dog, new-tricks one."

"Oh, Gina. Yeah." Colin's face grew wistful, and then he brightened. "We were just two ships passing in the night."

"Lovely," Bruce said, discovering that his normal male interest in Colin's conquests and escapades was simply not present today.

"Oh, she was lovely," Colin said, Bruce's irony lost on him. "The type of woman who is ideal—she was as much the 'love 'em and leave 'em' kind as me. Adventurous, too. I mean the positions—"

"TMI," Bruce inserted quickly, stopping Colin before he really got rolling. "Too much information. Sex is not a spectator sport."

"It could have been." Colin grinned widely.

"Ugh!" Bruce drained the scotch. "So you think the jury will come back in your favor?"

Colin's expression sobered. "I believe so. That information you pointed me toward really helped. I didn't think old McGregor had a whammy in him, but I have to admit that he dropped a bomb."

"He's a good lawyer. That's the number-one rule in this business. Never underestimate your opposing counsel. Always remember that the case is like a huge chess match and that you have to think through every possible move and have a contingency plan for the one move you might have missed."

"Check, but no checkmate."

"Exactly." Bruce pushed the empty tumbler toward

the lounge's cocktail waitress. "No, thanks. I'm fine," he said to her offer of another.

"Only one?" Colin arched an eyebrow.

Bruce might have had two drinks total over the course of an evening, but not tonight, especially when he wasn't going to be eating anything until later. Colin had already been late in arriving, and it was nearly time to leave to meet Christina. "I'm going to cut out of here early. I can't stay for dinner. Other plans."

"You're on call?"

"No. I told Christina I'd meet her for dinner. We're going to discuss the case."

"You dog. All this crap about not thinking she was hot. Where are you taking her? Into Batesville? The Sherman House has great atmosphere and food. The Chateaubriand for two is great, as is the Filet Oscar."

"We're going to McDonald's."

"Where's that?" It took a moment, and then Colin sputtered as he realized exactly what Bruce had said. "As in the golden arches? You're taking her out for a Big Mac? You're kidding me."

"Nope." Bruce suppressed some laughter at his friend's expense. The idea did seem pretty hysterical. "We're going to discuss the case over fast food while her daughter runs amok in the play area."

"Oh, good grief," Colin said, disgust evident. "Kids always spoil everything, don't they?"

"It means that she's off-limits, so I won't have to hire your sorry ass to defend mine," Bruce said. Bella would make a good chaperon and remind Bruce that no matter how pretty Christina may have been today in her Prada suit, she was not even an option. Although the idea of a woman with a child didn't seem so repugnant anymore. Not when it was Christina. Maybe he'd been narrow-minded about a few things. He stood up quickly. "I'm going to leave. If not, I'll be late."

"Yeah, yeah." Colin shook his head. "I'm going to eat alone."

Bruce pointed and Colin turned his attention to where two of their former high-school classmates sat, wineglasses in hand. Both women were newly divorced. "Marti Jenson and Carla Lane are over in the corner giggling about something. You could always join them."

"Go," Colin ordered.

"Be safe," Bruce said.

"Always," Colin answered, and Bruce left the lounge, knowing Colin well enough to know that he would be safe. They'd lost one of their close friends at sixteen to a drunk driver, and as much as it might be fun to occasionally tie one on, neither Bruce nor Colin ever went over the legal limit if they were driving.

Besides, a DWI wasn't good behavior for anyone. Not only had Lancaster and Morris handled several wrongful death lawsuits for victims' families, but Bruce had also seen enough mangled cars when the fire department had responded to motor vehicle accidents. Those sights took a while to forget.

"Bruce," a woman's voice called.

Bruce paused and turned. Standing in the country-club foyer was Elaine Gray. "Elaine."

She still had on the navy suit she'd worn earlier that day, but she'd now tucked her platinum blond hair behind her ears, softening the style. She clutched a small handbag. "I didn't realize you'd be here tonight."

"Morrisville's a small world."

"That it is." She gestured to the coat he had draped over his arm. "Are you leaving? I'd love to talk to you about what you brought to my attention today."

"We have a meeting next week, don't we?" Bruce tossed the words she'd used that morning back at her.

Her congenial expression didn't change at his barb. "Bruce. I would never guess you'd be one to pass up an opportunity. Would it entice you more to know that I'm buying?"

He merely raised his eyebrows at her and waited. Her expression turned wry.

"You sure know how to make it hard on a girl. How about if I say my father's here and I've been filling him in on what you've been telling me. Will that sway you? A little informal powwow? After all, isn't that how most business really gets done?"

The big hand on the Roman-numeral clock just above the club's ornate double doors inched toward six. Bruce didn't have Christina's cell phone number. Damn. Elaine had him, and she knew it. "I can stay only a few minutes," he said.

Elaine smiled sweetly. "Follow me."

# Chapter Six

He was late. Christina tapped her watch, as if the movement of her forefinger would somehow make the watch on her left wrist roll back from reading 6:26.

Even Kyle hadn't had the indecency to stand her up. Cheat on her, yes, but for the most part, he hadn't left her waiting in a McDonald's restaurant with a bunch of legal briefs spread out over a booth table during dinner rush. Luckily, she'd gone home and changed—at least she didn't appear even more out of place in Prada when everyone else wore jeans.

She'd tried to tune out her surroundings and work, but all around her kids shrieked their way through various tunnels suspended from the ceiling. Bella was having the time of her life.

Other mothers were there, and some were reading. Almost every mother in the PlayPlace wore a gold band on her left hand. Christina instead wore a blue sapphire set in white gold, which she'd bought to keep her ring finger from feeling naked once the ostentatious wed-

ding set had gone into a safe deposit box just in case
Bella wanted it someday. After all, Bella's daddy had
loved her mother once, even if only for a brief time.

Christina pushed the papers aside. She could read the
things at home. When Bella raced up to take a quick sip
of her apple juice, Christina told her, "Five more minutes."

"Mom…" Bella began.

"Five minutes," Christina repeated. Bella's face fell
briefly. Then she dashed back into the tunnels, and
within seconds Christina heard her daughter again
shrieking with delight.

Christina thumbed through the legal briefs one final
time, then simply gave up. She had little concentration
left at this point. Just where was Bruce? She hardly
knew the man, and during the little time they had, he'd
annoyed her and gotten on her nerves at least half of it.

But despite his flaws, she wouldn't wish him into a
ditch or anything like that. Hopefully, that was not what
had happened tonight. She pushed thoughts of where
he could be out of her mind. She'd had to learn to do
that with Kyle. Thinking too much and speculating on
the unknown could drive a person insane.

As the middle child, she'd grown up being over-
looked—overshadowed by her brother's sports prow-
ess and by her baby sister's cleverness. Kyle had
overshadowed Christina, as well. How often had she
stood behind him while he'd hogged the media spot-
light? That nagging feeling of self-doubt, that innate
sense of invading doom caused by a partner's unfaith-
fulness, had driven Christina to believe that she wasn't

good enough, and that, had she been stronger, prettier, more something, her husband wouldn't have strayed. She'd conquered that finally and after many long years had left Kyle Jones behind.

But Bruce wasn't her husband. She shouldn't care for him, wonder where he was, worry whether he was okay. She didn't know him that well.

Irrespective of his easy demeanor with the kids at the elementary school and his sexy grin, she had to focus on the fact that he was just a colleague, and he'd managed life fine so far by himself. She refused to be attracted to him, so why was she concerned about his welfare and not furious and angry? Had his powerful charm gotten to her already?

There were worse things than being alone, and one was caring for a man who would never care for you. She would never let her heart be damaged again. Best just to leave Bruce in that box labeled "work colleague" and not try to move him into one marked "friend."

For some reason, though, like a craving for chocolate cake, she wanted to get to know Bruce. Yet the risks might be too high.

"Bella, time," Christina called, relieved that her daughter instantly complied, exited the tunnels and began to put on her shoes. Christina loaded up her briefcase and drew on her coat. Bella had just finished zipping her coat, when a glance outside revealed that a huge black pickup truck had just entered the parking lot.

"Let's go," Christina said, her sudden urge to escape

overwhelming her. Fighting with Bruce again was not a path she wanted to tread tonight.

"'Bye, everyone," Bella called.

"Bella, please," Christina said. One hand held her car keys and briefcase, and the other she stretched out. Bella's warm fingers interlocked with hers, and Christina made a beeline for the playroom exit, using her hip against the crash bar to open the door.

They'd gotten through the restaurant and to the exit door opposite of Bruce's truck, when she heard his voice. "Christina?"

There was no way she could pretend not to have heard him. She clutched Bella's hand a little tighter and slowly turned around. "Bruce. What a surprise." Sarcasm she couldn't resist dripped from her voice. "Did you get lost?"

"No." His grin was infectious and charming, but Christina refused to waver, especially in light of the curious speculation of a few interested onlookers.

"Have you eaten?" Bruce asked, offering no apology for his late arrival.

Her lips thinned. "Of course we've eaten. We've been here for forty minutes. Waiting," she added haughtily, just to be sure he'd get the point. "Now we're leaving."

Bella's eyes had widened. "You're that fireman," she said. "From my school. My friends all called you a hunk. Mama, what's a hunk?"

Christina wanted to drop through the floor as mirth entered Bruce's blue eyes. "Yep," Bruce answered easily, directing his heart-melting smile toward her daughter. "I'm the firefighter."

"Bella, we have to leave. You need your sleep tonight."

"I'm not tired," Bella announced, obviously fascinated by Bruce's arrival.

"Yes, but you are due for a bath tonight," Christina reminded Bella sharply.

"Let me get some food and we'll talk," Bruce interceded. "Despite having been at the club since five, I haven't eaten anything but one cold chicken wing."

She blinked, as if that motion would somehow clear her ears. Surely she'd misheard him. He'd stood her up because he'd been at the club? The country club, where he'd originally wanted to take her?

She peered at him. Bruce still wore the same suit he'd had on all day. He didn't seem to have been imbibing at a happy hour. She found her backbone. Where he'd been didn't matter. If he wasn't in a ditch, he had no excuses for being late, especially when he hadn't even had the courtesy to apologize. "We're going," Christina said firmly. "I have to get Bella home."

He shrugged. "Fine. I'll meet you at your place immediately after I grab something to go."

The thought of Bruce even knowing where she lived sent raw panic through her. Her little cottage was her personal haven. "No."

"We have to talk," he said, his tone now commanding. He cupped her elbow, the heat of his touch finding its way through the fabric of her coat. "I just met with Elaine and Donald Gray."

That statement got her attention and she jerked herself out of his reach. "You met with the Grays without me?"

"Well, yeah." He gave her a boyish grin that, despite its width, missed the mark.

Her first case and already he was working behind her back. So much for a truce. He hadn't wanted her to join the firm in the first place. He had effectively defined her job that afternoon, stereotyping her as sidekick.

She'd kick him all right. Smack on the rear—

Christina resisted the urge to ram the heel of her boot into his big toe. "I can't believe you had a meeting without me! Donald Gray never takes meetings, you told me!"

"He doesn't. It wasn't like that…."

How many times had Kyle said those words? Old patterns of behavior reared their ugly heads, clouding Christina's normally rational judgment. She cut off his explanation and reacted with gut instinct. "Of course it wasn't. Typical man. Leave the female at home, or in this case McDonald's, while you go off and take care of business. I am competent, Bruce, and you should treat me as such. None of this 'you Tarzan, me Jane' crap. I can forage quite fine and defend myself from wild beasts all on my very own. I am capable of saving myself. No man has to do it."

"I never said…" he protested.

Tiny fingers tugged on Christina's, reminding her of exactly where they were and that little ears were present. "We are going home now," she said, this time in her most forceful tone. "Alone. You and I can discuss this situation tomorrow in the office, where it's private." *And I'm much calmer,* she didn't add.

"Christina."

"I'm not listening," Bella commented.

But Christina would have none of it. Obviously, Bruce was alive and well. No emergency had kept him; instead, he'd been out schmoozing, trying to cut deals and undermining the very work she'd been brought in to do—as his superior, nonetheless!

"In the morning," she repeated for emphasis.

With that, she turned on her heel and left Bruce standing there, his jaw dropped in complete disbelief.

BRUCE GRABBED the brown plastic tray and headed for the table. Infernal woman. No woman had ever walked out on him, yet Christina had done it without even a good-bye. Ms. Boxing Gloves had certainly knocked him about.

But he wasn't down for the count. Far from it. Bruce Lancaster didn't go down over any woman.

Heck, it wasn't as though he had arranged the meeting without her, and he hadn't had her cell phone number. One had to take any opportunities dropped into one's lap.

If he was the typical male she'd stereotyped him as, then she was the typical female. She thought she made all the rules and had the prerogative to change them at any time without notice. Bruce had been tried and convicted for a crime he hadn't known he'd committed.

Of course, he'd done pretty much the same thing to her this morning. He winced at that mistake. Had it really been not even twenty-four hours since he'd found out that Christina Jones, the hot number in the genie costume who'd accidentally set off the elementary-school fire alarm, was his new senior partner and, technically, his superior?

In the short period he'd known her, how had she thrown him for a loop?

He had to admit he liked her verve. She did what few women dared. She stood up to him. She challenged him. While they weren't off to a very good start, she did intrigue him.

He began to unwrap the quarter-pound burger. He also admired her. Picking up and moving to a small town like Morrisville, Indiana, where everyone had known everyone since birth, had to be hard.

Bruce had grown up here, so he didn't feel any culture shock. And he'd had his job handed to him. Christina hadn't worked much, and this job was probably important to her, even if she didn't need the money to survive. It made her independent. He winced. She'd referred to herself as inferior, a Jane to his Tarzan. Not good. Was that how her ex had viewed her? Bruce decided that he'd eat crow later if that was what it took to appease Christina. And he wouldn't be making friends just because Reginald said for him to. Christina deserved better, and Bruce was determined to be more considerate at all times.

For now, though, hot food awaited. Bruce took a bite and savored the flavor of meat and melted cheese. He'd never be anything but a carnivore, and tonight he wasn't going to worry about his arteries.

As he chewed, he gazed through the soundproof

glass at the kids in the playroom. He assumed that was where Christina had eaten, alone. No, not quite alone. She'd had Bella.

Bruce was alone: no one sat at the table with him. However, he'd long gotten used to it—a man didn't have to be part of a twosome to enjoy sitting down at a table for a meal.

Yes, Christina had Bella. She would never be truly alone, even after Bella grew up and moved away.

That was what family was about. Having someone who was always there. He could see how close Bella and Christina were, and their bond had raised Christina in his esteem. He wanted a wife who would be just as committed to their child as Christina was to hers.

Bruce piled three French fries into his mouth. He'd always dreamed of having a huge family, unlike his own. His young sister had died of SIDS at four months. Bruce had been four when it had occurred, and his parents had never attempted to have more children.

Colin, however, had three sisters, and his house had been absolute chaos compared with the quiet, studious atmosphere of Bruce's. Growing up, Bruce had been at the Morris abode more than at his own house.

Bruce finished the French fries and moved the red paperboard container aside. He could understand Christina's frustration with him now that he thought about it. Plus, he hadn't apologized for being late. He'd been a real cad.

He grimaced. He'd made more missteps in one day with this woman than he had with all the others in his life combined. He hadn't gotten one thing correct from the moment he and Christina had met. That fact ate at him. He liked her, and he wouldn't have treated anyone this way. He'd really screwed up.

He'd apologize and explain everything to Christina tomorrow morning. The meeting with the Grays hadn't been much, a lot of sizing up of opponents, with questions like, "Is Lancaster and Morris really serious about pursuing this?" and "How dare you file with the EEOC?"

Bruce had assured them that his firm was serious in their demands. As per EEOC procedures, Lancaster and Morris had requested the "right to sue" letter the day it had filed the complaints. If consensus and settlement could not be reached, the EEOC was planning to step aside and let private litigation take the Title VII violations to federal court. By filing the letter along with the complaints, the official court filing could occur the moment the EEOC stepped aside. Donald Gray's genial face had never lost its poker quality, but Bruce had known the older man was ticked.

Bruce finished his burger and washed it down with pop. Most people didn't understand the law, and it was even more complicated when a federal agency was involved. The majority of civil cases never reached trial. Basically, if the lawyers for both parties could reach agreements, then the judges simply rubber-stamped those agreements and the court clerk filed them, making everything legally binding. Civil cases were like divorces—very few went to actual trial, although things could get ugly and expensive as legal missives flew back and forth.

Bruce's cell phone began to shrill. He frowned when he saw a number he didn't recognize. He flipped the phone open. "Bruce Lancaster."

"Bruce, this is Bob Orf down at Cyntech. I'm the director of environmental affairs. We've had a spill and it's big. Our first responders are on the scene, and we've notified OSHA and the EPA. County EMS is en route. We're going to evacuate the surrounding area to a three-mile radius just to be on the safe side."

Bruce bit back an instinctive curse. Every manufacturing plant's nightmare was to spill chemicals necessary to do the job. Cyntech had a big old tank, and Bruce had a sneaking suspicion that the ancient tank had somehow ruptured. Assessing liability and getting to any potential litigants before the ambulance chasers was Bruce's job, since he was the lawyer Cyntech kept on retainer.

"I'll be on my way as soon as I call in and let Lancaster and Morris know what's happening," Bruce said.

"Great." The man's relief was palpable. "Luckily, almost everything around us is farmland. The spill will affect very few people."

Bruce pressed End, made a quick call to Reginald and apprised him of the situation. "More than likely I'll be away for a few weeks," Bruce said. "Christina can handle the work with Angela. She did great today. However, I need to tell her what's going on. I didn't get her home number."

He reached into his jacket pocket and yanked out the small notebook and pen he kept there. "Go ahead. By the way, do you know where she lives? It might just be easier to go over there on my way to Cyntech."

"Looks like no sleep for you tonight," Reginald said. "She lives at 324 Maple Street. On the outskirts of town."

Which meant only five minutes away. Bruce snapped the notebook and the phone closed. He and Christina were about to have that talk tonight whether she liked it or not.

"MAMA, WHY WERE YOU yelling at that man?"

Christina rubbed the towel on Bella's dark-blond hair. Her daughter had just finished a shower and was dressed in her favorite pair of silk teddy-bear pajamas. "We weren't yelling."

"Yes, you were," Bella said matter-of-factly as her bare toes curled into the pink bathmat. "You sounded like you did when you didn't know I broke the good vase on accident. Angry."

Christina removed the towel and hung it to dry on the towel bar. She reached for a comb and the hair dryer. "Sometimes adults get angry with each other."

Bella's brown eyes revealed her confusion. "But why were you yelling at the fireman?"

"He's not a fireman." Christina paused. Good grief. How to explain. "Well, he is a fireman. But he's also a lawyer. We work together."

"At your new job?"

"Exactly. At my new job. And we're working on a

case together and we had some disagreements over it."
Christina began to comb out Bella's tangles.

"Does that mean you'll leave him?"

"Leave him?" Where had that come from? She wasn't with Bruce enough to leave him.

Bella tugged her head a little out of Christina's reach so that she could see her mother. "Well, you left Daddy, and Daddy had a disagreement with Elanna and he left her. I liked her. She wasn't as snotty as some of the other ones."

Christina bristled. Christina resolved to talk with her ex-husband at the next opportunity about his revolving-door women.

"No, sweetheart, I wasn't leaving him. We just have to learn how to become friends. Sometimes it takes adults a little longer than it does kids. With adults, things can be complicated." Christina turned her daughter back around and began to comb Bella's hair again.

Complicated—an understatement where Bruce Lancaster was concerned. The man was under her skin, and Christina really couldn't say why. Despite her being annoyed as all get-out, warring with Bruce Lancaster had a raw invigoration to it that simply enticed. Christina couldn't quite describe the feeling, except it was a little like the time she'd jumped off a cliff into the ocean. That had been on a dare from her cousins after they'd all made the jump during a family vacation in Mexico.

There had been fear and anxiety, yet at the same time there had been a thrill, and that, not her cousins' teasing, was what had compelled her to risk the unknown.

She'd jumped, and as her feet had hit the cool water, she'd felt strangely alive.

Bruce made her feel like that—made her want to lower her walls and risk again. Risk what, though? Christina wasn't sure exactly. Maybe risk ignoring all the rules she'd laid out for herself.

"I made lots of new friends tonight," Bella said, not noticing her mother's sudden contemplativeness. "Maybe it is easier for kids. Like with Megan."

"Exactly," Christina said. She turned on the blow dryer, and she and Bella sang songs during the five-minute hair-drying process. It was too cold to let Bella's hair stay wet the way she liked it. In the summer, Christina let Bella's long hair dry naturally. Finally her daughter's hair was acceptable for bed. "Time to brush your teeth," Christina announced. As she reached for the toothpaste, she frowned. Like this morning, was that her doorbell?

Christina experienced an odd sense of déjà vu. But it was now after seven-thirty in the evening and it was dark out. The insistent shrilling was indeed her doorbell, and after a half minute, she realized that whoever was at her door wasn't going to go away. "Brush your teeth, honey, then go climb in bed. I'll be back to check on you and read your story in a minute."

Christina went downstairs and flipped on the light switches as she entered the foyer. Her front door had a long, oval, etched-glass inset, and she could see a large shape on the other side. Besides ringing the doorbell, whoever was there was pounding on the door. Her shoulders slumped in resignation, as if she'd known exactly who it was before he called, "Christina, we have to talk. It's cold out here! Open up!"

She tossed the dead bolt and undid the lock on the knob. "Hello, Bruce," she said as she opened the door. "Considering I said tomorrow morning at the office, what brings you by now?"

"Emergency," he answered, bulldozing by her and stepping into the foyer. Her sarcastic "Make yourself at home" died on her lips when he added, "I wanted to tell you myself that I'm going to be out of the office for about two weeks."

Cold November air swirled around her feet, and Christina quickly shut the door. "What?"

He gestured with his gloved hands. "Cyntech had a spill. I'm their lawyer, and I've got to go do liability control. I'm going to be on-site as soon as I leave here."

"You're…"

"Working all through the night, yes." He must have seen that she didn't quite understand the situation. "I'm going to be at Cyntech's facility, working with their management on how to best limit their liability. Watch your news later tonight. I'm sure the spill will make it. Nothing happens around here, and the evacuation area has a three-mile radius. OSHA's also on the way. I'll try to check in with Angela daily, and she knows how to reach me. Have her give you all my numbers. I've worked from the field before, so it'll be fine. Just follow the directions I send."

"You're going to issue directions on a case that you aren't even working on?"

He exhaled a sigh of frustration. "Christina, I'm not questioning your competence. You'll need this week just to get up to speed. I'll take care of rescheduling the Morrisville Garment meeting. I'm sure that after tonight they'll appreciate the favor."

"Oh, yes, your meeting," she snapped.

"An impromptu meeting that wasn't scheduled," he retorted. "Are you always this difficult?"

"No. I'm worse," she shot back.

"Figured." He moved toward her, his boots heavy on the hardwood floor, but she didn't budge. This was her house. He couldn't... His blue eyes darkened and adrenaline shot through her. It was as though he was seeing her for the first time. "You are the most impossible woman that I've ever met."

"I'm sure that's a good thing," she said, trying to keep her voice light as the moment changed into something she recognized but didn't want to give credence to.

"I think it's a very dangerous thing," Bruce said, his voice husky. "In one day you have turned my world upside down."

"It wasn't intentional," she said, tugging on the hem of the long-sleeved T-shirt she wore.

"And neither was my being late," he told her smoothly. "It just happened."

He had her. "You *are* a good lawyer," she said, amazed and more than a little mesmerized by where he was going with this. The air hummed, and not because of the warm air forced up through the floor vents. Her body, inches from his, reacted with surprising desire.

Hormones. Pheromones. Too much self-induced celibacy. A woman had needs, too, and when she and Kyle had first been married, Christina had fulfilled them all. She'd been without for a long time. That was what this sudden awareness of Bruce Lancaster, this desire for this man, was. She took a step back. Unexplained passion was not acceptable. She had to work with him.

"I'm sorry for tonight," Bruce said, his gloved hand catching hers. The leather was soft against her fingertips. "I didn't mean to leave you alone. I'm not going to offer you any excuse. I know when to apologize. I was wrong. I'm sorry you were alone and waiting."

"I'm used to it," she said.

"No, you should never be waiting," he said. "Not a woman like you."

Oh, God! To hear those words from any other man! But Bruce Lancaster was fire, and she wanted safe and sedate. Kyle had been volatile. This time she desired normal. Time to regain control. She had way too much to lose if she didn't. She couldn't let herself be swept away ever again and off the new course she'd chosen for her life.

She removed her hand and in an instant rebuilt the wall that his touch had brought down. "But I will be waiting, Bruce. For your orders. On the case. Unless by your admission I shouldn't wait. I should take the ball and run with it."

He laughed, his chuckle a mix of pain and pleasure. "Oh, you're a good lawyer, too. You almost got me there."

"I don't think I'm trying to get you," she said.

"Yes, you are. You want me to view you as competent, and trust me, Christina, I do. There's no doubt in my mind that you're a top-notch lawyer. You have a legal mind that can challenge mine, and damn, that's rare. Heck, fighting with you captivates me. I can't make one step around you without thinking every angle through. If I say you're beautiful, will it be unwanted harassment? You certainly aren't a Jane to my Tarzan, but I have to admit you pull something totally primitive out of me, and I don't even know you. You aren't my protégée, yet I'm determined to teach you everything you need to know in law, even though in the future I'm sure somehow you'll trounce me with it. I'm damned if I do, damned if I don't, Christina Jones, who wears boxing gloves and wants to knock me down. Well, you've landed some blows. I'm definitely reeling."

"I'm sure it's just stress," Christina said, trying to process Bruce's double meaning. "This has been a lousy day for both of us. I'm sorry I made that comment. Getting divorced has been hard, what with everyone pulling on me in one direction or another. I had no right to take any of my life situations or my preconceived notions out on you."

"Fate can be cruel and she can be kind. The jury is still out on which way our relationship will go. But I'm in for the ride, and certainly not down for the count."

She frowned. What exactly did he mean by that? If she ventured the wrong guess... He wasn't going to tell her. Instead he'd walked to the door.

"I'll be in touch, Christina. And not to bellow my orders at you. Just let me know what you're doing, okay?"

"With the case," Christina confirmed.

"Of course," Bruce said, a little too smoothly. He reached for the doorknob, and for the first time, Christina noticed that the Bruce who all day had been totally confident, even condescending, appeared a little shaken and unsure of himself. Perhaps it was just tiredness. He was, after all, not going to get any sleep tonight.

"Mama, are you going to read to me now?" Bella called.

"Just a minute, honey," Christina said, turning toward the stairs. When she turned around, a gust of cold air greeted her.

"Good night, Christina," Bruce said as he stepped out the door and closed it behind him. Within moments she heard his big diesel pickup rumble off.

What exactly had happened here tonight? How had things changed and somehow gotten out of control?

"Mama," Bella called.

Christina pushed Bruce from her mind. She couldn't think about that now. And if she was smart, not ever.

As Bruce drove to Cyntech, he couldn't believe what had happened. Well, nothing had happened. At least, nothing that Christina would ever know about.

He'd walked into her house, and something had changed almost immediately. Maybe it was the way she'd stood there in only a pair of jeans and a long-sleeved white T-shirt that had clung to her breasts. Maybe it had been her bare feet, each toenail painted with hot-red nail polish. Maybe it was the way her blond hair had draped over her shoulders, the up-turned ends dancing exactly where his fingers suddenly itched to be.

But stepping into Christina's house and simply see-ing her at the end of the day had been akin to a slap in the face. Her standing there in the foyer had hinted of domesticity, a domesticity that he'd suddenly craved.

Christina Jones was more than under his skin. In her foyer, he'd wanted nothing more than to draw her into his arms, carry her upstairs and discover exactly what her bed looked like.

Not a wise move for two people having to work on a harassment case together. But the temptation had been there, and he hadn't read her face wrong, either. He'd been right about Bella's being a good chaperon.

The truck easily covered the distance to Cyntech. The firefighters blocking the county highway recog-nized him and let him through as soon as he'd put on a HAZMAT suit. Within two minutes Bruce approached Cyntech's main gate. The guard identified him, let him through and radioed ahead.

Work was always good, Bruce thought, as he stepped out of the truck and adjusted his oxygen tank. Work gave a man a purpose, something to keep his mind off his troubles.

For Bruce Lancaster had just realized that where Christina Jones was concerned, he had very deep trou-bles indeed.

## Chapter Seven

"How are you doing?"

"I'm great, actually." Christina pushed aside the legal brief and watched as Angela walked into the small conference room, a six-inch stack of file folders nestled in her arms. Perhaps *waddled* into the room was a more apt description, Christina thought. Angela appeared to have become rounder overnight as she inched closer to her delivery date. In Christina's final months of pregnancy with Bella, she'd been unable to see her feet or tie her tennis shoes.

"I've just finished the last of the court decisions I needed to read," Christina said. She eyed the folders. "Are those all for me?"

"Unfortunately, yes. I've got the individual files on each of the women in the suit right here. We haven't taken formal depositions, only informal statements. Bruce wants you to read through all these by Monday afternoon."

Surely he didn't expect her to work over the weekend. It was already Friday, and in a sense it had been a peaceful four days. Christina had gotten a lot of work done. "Did he call?" she asked.

"About an hour ago to check in," Angela admitted. "He had only a few minutes."

"Ah," Christina said with a glance at her watch. It was three in the afternoon. Ever since Bruce had visited her Monday night, he hadn't talked to her directly, instead simply issuing directives on the case through Angela, as he'd said he would do.

The first time, Angela had given Christina a sympathetic smile, told her that Bruce was up to his ears in work at Cyntech and that he'd be back soon. By now Christina was used to the situation. "Any idea when he'll return?" she asked.

"End of next week, middle of the following. Did you see him on TV last night? He's quite a spokesman, isn't he?"

"He did well," Christina admitted. Not only had Bruce's dazzling smile had the young female reporter practically preening in front of him, but he'd also likely endeared himself to the masses by using plain talk anyone could understand. Watching him, she'd found herself awed. If he could tug at her with his sincerity, she could only imagine the reaction of those who didn't know him.

"He is good," Angela concurred, her admiration for her boss evident. "Yesterday I sent everyone affected by the evacuation five-hundred-dollar appreciation checks. Even though people were only indisposed for less than five hours and no utilities were turned off, the amount covers any inconvenience they may have suffered."

"A preemptive strike."

"Pretty much. Cyntech is a large employer around here, and people in this rather shaky economy of late are grateful to have jobs there. The company's union and pays well. A goodwill gesture like this will go a long way toward defusing any community anger."

"While still not admitting liability," Christina said, impressed. Bruce's preemptive strike would work wonders, effectively eliminating any civilian lawsuits. "I'm sure there was a carefully worded letter with the checks," Christina added.

"Typed and photocopied myself and couriered over," Angela said. "Cashing the checks means they agree."

Christina shook her head, her dark-blond hair swishing around her shoulders. She'd worn it loose the past few days. "So with the residents appeased, Bruce can turn his attention to negotiating with the federal regulators."

"He'll have to. Cyntech's bound to be subject to some pretty hefty fines. It all remains to be worked out," Angela said. "Well, here are the files. I'll be leaving a few minutes early. It's my anniversary tonight."

"Congratulations."

"Thanks. We're driving into Batesville for dinner. I'll see you Monday. TGIF—Thank God It's Friday. I'll get the whole weekend to sleep. I need it. The baby's been keeping me up all night by kicking!"

"I remember that," Christina said. "Have fun tonight and try to get some rest this weekend."

After Angela left, Christina reached for the file folders. By the time she'd finished reading the fifth one, a common thread had emerged.

All the women at the factory were trying to make a better life for themselves. All of them still hadn't caught a break, except for the fact that, unlike a lot of others, they had green cards that made them legal.

An idea began to form in the back of Christina's mind. The more she thought about it, the more she liked it. She decided not to let the fact that Bruce probably wouldn't approve bother her. She was the senior partner here, and she could make decisions, especially if Cyntech would be demanding his attention. She'd run her plan by Reginald just for good measure, but only once her arrangements were almost a done deal.

As for Bruce, she'd deal with him later.

THURSDAY, NOVEMBER 18. Bruce tore off his 365 Golf-Holes-A-Day calendar to the proper page. Going into his office to work felt odd. First, he'd been out in Indianapolis most of the year, and then he'd barely been back in the office for half a day before being whisked away by Cyntech.

Sure, he'd stopped by the office, usually late at night, long after everyone was gone. But he hadn't worked, or done any housekeeping at that time, like changing calendars. He'd stopped by only to make sure things didn't build up at Lancaster and Morris while he was at his temporary office at Cyntech.

Every day Angela had couriered over to him whatever he'd needed and forwarded important phone messages. He would read over everything, make notations, send it all back and then she'd sort it out. It was a system they'd perfected over the years they'd worked together. The only difference this time was that he dropped the stuff on her desk himself.

"Good morning," Angela said as she entered. "I see you're here bright and early."

"I wanted to get caught up," Bruce replied before glancing up. Angela wore a very colorful maternity dress today. "I've been trying to find the profile folders on the Morrisville Garment case. I didn't see them in the conference room."

"Christina has them. I think she took them to her office. She's been working mainly from there."

He frowned. While it was logical for Christina to work in her office, especially since it had windows and a view, he'd set up the conference room as a home base for the duration of the case. He hadn't communicated with her since leaving, having trusted her to follow his directives. After that rough first day and that sexually charged evening, he'd figured that it would be better for both of them if they gave each other some much-needed space.

Not that having time away had changed anything. Now that he was back in the office, the first thing he'd wanted to do was see Christina. He restrained himself. He'd never acted liked a schoolboy and didn't plan on starting now.

"You had a call from Elaine Gray to confirm the date of the rescheduled meeting. She wants you to phone her personally."

"I can do that." Bruce scratched the note on the pad. "Next Monday, right?"

"Yes."

"Did you tell Christina?"

"That's why Elaine wants you to confirm personally. Christina talked to her last week to set up the meeting."

"She had a conversation with Elaine Gray? I didn't leave instructions for that. Why would she have called her?"

Angela was already backing toward the door. "You'll have to ask her."

With a legitimate excuse to see Christina, Bruce stood. "I think I will."

But when he reached Christina's office, she wasn't there. She wasn't there an hour later, either, when the clock ticked past nine-thirty. Since the offices at Lancaster and Morris were never locked, he took a minute to stand in the doorway.

She'd personalized the room since that first day. Crayon drawings were tacked to the oversize bulletin board now adorning one wall. Portraits of Bella at various ages lined the bookshelves and held dominant space on Christina's desk. Bruce stepped farther into the room. A few pieces of clay pottery, obviously shaped by a child's hand, had prominent places on a shelf. But it was the glimpse of one framed picture that drew him across the room and had him stepping behind her desk, the file folders he'd come searching for temporarily forgotten.

He lifted the frame so he could better see the

photo. It had to have been taken shortly after Bella's birth, but not much more than a week. Bruce hadn't had much experience around newborns, but he'd seen Colin's sisters' children within a week or two of their births.

Bella rested in her mother's arms, her face angelic in sleep. She'd lost that ruddy color of the first few newborn days. Her cheeks were still baby full and her nose pug, as if her head hadn't yet elongated from being scrunched during birth. Her little red lips had thinned into a relaxed line, and her downy hair stood in tufts. Already one could tell the beauty of Bella. It was there in the smooth, soft face that expressed innocence and trust and the innate belief that the woman who held her, Christina, would always love her and treasure her.

Bruce hadn't ever seen this Christina before. Sure, she was eight years younger and her blond hair was a lot longer, but that wasn't what he noticed. No, her face radiated happiness. There were no lines of stress, no hidden metaphorical boxing gloves, no circles of tiredness underneath her brown eyes.

The photograph had captured her as fresh, soft and untarnished by betrayal.

Irrationally, he found himself angry. Despite his own personal beef with Christina, he could never imagine cheating on the joyous woman in this photograph. If Christina had been his wife, he wouldn't have treated her the way Kyle Jones had. She was a woman to be treasured, even now. He wasn't sure where this proprietary streak came from, especially when he was not happy that she'd deliberately called Elaine Gray and conveniently forgotten to relay the message.

Nevertheless, he found himself wanting to be her champion.

"What are you doing here?"

Bruce put the photograph down quickly, as if it had burned his fingers. "Colin," Bruce said as he tried to get any perception of being caught at something under-handed out of his posture. "What are you doing here?"

"My office is two doors down."

Bruce didn't like the sound of that. "So you've been coming by and bugging Christina?"

Colin stepped back a pace. "Actually, I've missed her most days, and still haven't met her. I've been in court, remember? I've had back-to-back trials. Thought today might be the day I'd finally meet the new senior partner."

"She's not here," Bruce said flatly.

Colin seemed a bit put out. "That's obvious. But you are."

"I'm searching for some files that Angela said Christina took to her office," Bruce said, immensely relieved that Morrisville's resident playboy still hadn't met Christina. Heck, Bruce rationalized, his reaction was only because he and Colin were as close as brothers, and, knowing everything he did about the guy, Bruce wouldn't wish Colin on Christina. He was saving Christina from a menace, rather than he himself being jealous. The rationalizations made this new feeling of ownership more palatable. "I haven't found them yet."

"Maybe she took them home."

"That was going to be my next step, Sherlock. Find out where she is and why she isn't here." With that, Bruce walked past Colin and down the hallway toward Angela's desk.

"Christina's not here," Angela said immediately, as if reading Bruce's mind. "Bella's sick. Christina's working from home today. She called in a few minutes ago. I buzzed your office, but you weren't there."

He'd been in Christina's office. "Did she take the files home?"

"I don't know." Angela shrugged apologetically. "I had my neonatal appointment yesterday so I left early. Would you like me to call her and ask?"

Bruce's frustration mounted, but he inhaled a deep breath and calmed himself. He'd contact Christina himself. "Don't worry about it. I'll do it. How did your appointment go? Everything the way it should be?"

Angela smiled, that dreamy smile of a woman soon to see her child. "Everything's perfect."

"That's super," Bruce said, backing off before Angela got emotional. When Colin's sisters had been pregnant, they'd cried at Hallmark commercials and sad country-music videos. Hormones were dangerous things. "I'm going to try to catch up with Christina."

"Okay," Angela said. Bruce strode back to his office. He reached for the phone, then decided against dialing. Phones could be turned off, calls diverted to an answering machine. He buzzed Angela. "I'm going to Christina's to work. Call me on my cell if you need me."

"Will do," she replied, and within minutes Bruce was in his truck, on his way.

"WHAT ARE YOU DOING HERE?" Christina asked without preamble when she responded to the caller at her front door.

"Is that any way to greet me after me being away from the office for so long?" Bruce teased easily. He'd thrown her; her surprise was clearly readable. Her brown eyes had widened, a telltale flush had pinked her cheeks, and her lips had parted just so.

He inwardly groaned. Maybe he shouldn't be gazing at her lips. Even devoid of all glossy fabrication, they still had a subtle sheen to them that made him just want to flick his tongue over them and….

"You have some files I need," Bruce said, trying to return to seriousness and sanity. "And since you're not going to work today, I brought myself to you. I know…the sacrifices I make to make your life easier."

Christina inched the door open and allowed him to enter. "Come in quick. It's cold out. Bella's sick," she added.

"Angela told me," Bruce answered. Like the last time, Christina wore a faded pair of jeans. This time she'd topped them with a soft pink sweater set that Bruce recognized as cashmere. Her honey-colored hair was pulled back into an easy ponytail. As she stepped under the hall light, though, he noticed dark circles underneath her eyes. "How's she doing? You look like you had a long night."

Christina sighed. "Bella tossed and turned constantly, so I didn't get much sleep. She has what Megan recently finished. A virus."

"Symptoms?"

"Fever of 102, vomiting, although I think we're finished with that. Next we'll have to deal with the other end."

Bruce winced. Parenthood did have its less-glorious moments. "Can the doctor do anything for her?"

"I talked to him just before you showed up. He says to simply let the virus run its course. Give her lots of fluids, a bland diet. The usual. I'll go get those files for you. You're probably in a hurry."

"Nope. No rush. I've got time to spare. In fact, I was thinking that maybe we could just both work from here today, if that'd make things easier for you."

"Here?" Christina squeaked.

"Sure, why not? You've got the files, and I grabbed a few other things we might go over. Are you set up in your office?"

"Actually…" Christina pointed, and through the archway Bruce could see she'd piled everything into neat stacks on her dining-room table.

"Ah," he said, realizing he hadn't had a house tour. He didn't even know if she had an office. Last time he'd been here, he'd only stood in the foyer, wholly focused on Christina. That had been enough to shake him to his core.

Now he took a moment to study his surroundings. To his right was a small sitting room. It held two tall bookcases filled with leather-bound volumes, a Victorian love seat in a floral print that appeared uncomfortable and two wing chairs that didn't seem they'd be much better to sit on. The dining room, to his left, was double the size of the sitting room, but the dining room wasn't exactly huge, either. The mission-style table could seat six easily, but eight would be crowded. The room also contained a china cabinet.

Bruce suddenly remembered his package. He held up the large paper sack. "I brought bagels," he announced. "From Spencer's. Fresh baked this morning and guaranteed to be delicious."

"Asiago cheese bagels?" she asked hopefully.

"Plus blueberry and plain." Bruce could see she was tempted, so he upped the ante. "They make their own cream-cheese spreads. I've got low-fat strawberry, an apple butter and…"

Christina reached for the bag, and the paper crinkled as she took it from him. "Okay, go sit down in the dining room. You can stay, but only because you've brought food. What can I get you to drink? We have milk, water, orange and apple juice. Oh, and coffee. I've been drinking that by the gallon today. It's hazelnut flavored."

"A woman after my own heart," Bruce said. "Hazelnut coffee would be divine. It's one of my favorites."

She walked into the dining room and Bruce followed her. "Have a seat," she said.

He watched as she disappeared through another small archway. Curiosity about how far she'd gotten on the case had him lifting one edge of the file folder. And then, because he couldn't help himself, he ignored her notes and followed her. The kitchen was about five feet beyond a door that he guessed led to the basement. "Can I help you with anything?" he asked.

He'd startled her again and she jumped.

"I'm fine," she said, quickly regaining her poise. But Bruce still saw the shake to her hand as she set the last bagel on the serving plate. "Coffee cups are on that mug tree. Help yourself." She gestured with her elbow, indicating the location of the coffeepot. She removed the last of the spreads from the bag.

"I like your kitchen," Bruce said. The sand-washed cabinetry suited the small space, as did the matching granite countertop.

"It's small but well designed," Christina said. "The real estate agent told me the previous owners had it re-done. I didn't have to change a thing except for the dish towels. Even the dishwasher is high end. This was the best rental house I'd seen and it has an option to purchase."

"Do you miss it?" Bruce suddenly asked.

"Miss what?"

"The high life. You're in a three-bedroom house that's adorable, but can't be anything close to the man-sion you probably lived in."

Christina shrugged. "Yes, but even though it's just a rental, this house is mine. All mine. I never had much use for ostentation. I have yet to see someone drive more than one car or watch more than one TV at a time. By living here, I'm able to put part of Bella's child-support money into a trust fund for her."

Christina lifted a bagel and tore off a piece, which

she tossed, spreadless, into her mouth. She chewed and swallowed. "I don't want Bella growing up spoiled or too pampered. You see enough of those teenage divas on TV. Kyle can buy and give her anything except time. In the end, stuff is just stuff. I learned that when I walked away from it all. Once you take the chains of fear off, it's amazing how free you are and how much more you appreciate things."

"I wouldn't know," Bruce admitted as he processed what she'd disclosed. "I've never been in a situation I've hated that much."

"Not even being forced to be a lawyer instead of a full-time firefighter?"

Bruce contemplated that for a moment. "No, not even that. I love law, and I like what I do. So in a sense I have the best of both worlds. But I've always been free to do what I choose. If I'd really wanted to be a firefighter, my father and grandfather would have let me. My mother is overprotective and wouldn't like it, but she'd have given in. So I'm nothing to be admired. Unlike you."

"What do you mean?"

"You were obviously in a situation you didn't like and you removed yourself from it."

"It was more than not liking my circumstances. Leaving Kyle had to do with how he treated me and how he didn't respect me. Many people thought I was crazy. I mean, he didn't abuse me, per se. No hitting, slapping or anything like that. So everyone wondered what I was thinking by leaving him. 'Come on,' they said. 'Sports jocks and rock stars all cheat. Deal with it.' But I couldn't. That wasn't the marriage I wanted."

She carried the plate of bagels as if it were protective armor. "All my life I've had to deal with the expectation that I would be perfect. Kyle was another incarnation of that. The perfect provider, the incredible physical specimen. I lived in his shadow and conceded who I was, changing myself to his wishes. While I didn't have to walk five paces behind, what Kyle did was acceptable in his mind. His ego was first—his need for women, his desire for everything to be just so, his need for the limelight and adoration from everyone else. They came at my expense and my daughter's expense. I wanted my marriage to be normal. You know…that even though he was a star football player, we'd still have family dinners and family time. But in all honesty, I've learned that normal doesn't exist."

"I think normal is what you make of it. The Morris family was like that, though mine wasn't."

"Normal is an illusion," Christina said. "But it's an illusion that I want. Here, in this tiny kitchen that doesn't scream money and fame, I can at least pretend it exists. Bella should have a normal childhood, not be able to jet off to London or Paris on a minute's notice."

"I'm sorry," Bruce said all of a sudden, with a fierceness that came from somewhere deep.

"Don't be," Christina said with a resigned smile. She set the plate of bagels back down. "I have enough money, I now have a great job and I have a beautiful daughter. I see so much ugliness in the world that, trust me, I know how fortunate I am."

"You impress me," Bruce said quietly. He'd been so wrong about her from the beginning and he hated himself for it. "I'm sorry if I've misjudged you at any point."

"Accepted," she said, giving him the first true smile she'd ever directed at him. It knocked his socks off.

At that moment, Bruce understood exactly how much trouble Christina Jones could be. She was the type of woman a man could fall for. Hard.

But she was a woman who didn't want a man. Didn't desire one to come rescue her, toss her on his horse and carry her to his castle. She'd been there. Done that.

She wanted her own horse and castle. Disquiet stole over Bruce. What motivation did she have to try to love again? Being hurt once was bad enough.

"I hear Bella," she announced abruptly. "Why don't you take all this stuff into the dining room and I'll meet you there in a few minutes. I'm going to check on her."

About five minutes later, Christina traveled downstairs, a groggy Bella in her arms. Bruce stood.

"See, Mr. Lancaster is here," she said. "That's whose voice you heard."

"Bruce," he corrected.

"Bruce," Bella said, attempting a small smile. His heart went out to her. He could tell she ached all over.

"Bella's going to watch some television in the family room while we work. And I'm going to make her some toast."

"Plain bagel," Bella said, seeing the tray on the table.

"Okay, honey. I'll toast you a plain bagel. That will be fine, although you can't have anything on it."

Bella pouted but complied. Christina carried her into the family room, and Bruce followed. Here again, Christina's touches were visible. The room was only twelve by fourteen, but the two tall windows provided an excellent view of the tree-lined backyard. The room was decorated in warm earth tones and plaids, and Christina soon had Bella settled onto the sofa, a warm blanket wrapped around her daughter.

"It's time for her Tylenol," Christina said. "I'll go get it."

As she left, Bruce took a seat at the end of the couch. "So I hear Megan got you sick," he said.

Bella attempted a giggle but failed miserably and winced instead. "Uh-huh. She was out of school for three whole days. I have to get better because I'm seeing my dad next weekend. He doesn't like it when I'm sick."

"No?" Bruce said, for lack of anything better.

"No," Bella said. "It might make him sick, and he's got to play football. The Bengals might have a chance to play in the Super Bowl, but they can't do it without my dad."

"I see."

"I hate leaving Mommy alone for Thanksgiving. She's not going to Houston this year."

"She usually goes to Houston?" Even sick, Bella was a fountain of information.

"We usually go," Bella corrected as precociously as one who was ill could manage. "But she has dinner plans. So I have to get better. I'm hoping Mama doesn't catch what I have. She's a mom. Moms aren't allowed to get sick."

"I think your mom's pretty tough."

"Mama is tough," Bella said with a proud nod that brought on another wince.

"Then I'm predicting that she probably won't catch whatever bug you've got," Bruce said. He reached over and adjusted Bella's blanket. "Besides, she probably had it when she was a kid."

"Like chicken pox," Bella said. "You only get that once. I've never had it, but I got the shot."

"Exactly," Bruce said. He turned his head slightly. Christina was poised in the doorway, observing the exchange. "Here's your Tylenol," Bruce said.

Bella made a sour face.

"I also have your toasted bagel," Christina said, and Bella brightened upon hearing that.

Within a few moments, Bruce and Christina were seated across from each other at the dining-room table, the bagels and spreads between them.

"You're very good with her, you know," Bruce complimented her.

"Thank you," Christina said. "I wasn't in the beginning."

Bruce had been opening a file folder. He stopped and closed it again. "You're not serious."

"Actually, I am." Christina's ponytail bobbed as she gave a wistful smile. "You'd figure that in my huge family I'd be used to babies, but when I held Bella for the first time I was petrified. She was so tiny, and all mine to care for. Having a baby is a humbling experience. The world is no longer yours. You are second. Someone else's needs must come first, or she won't survive. You always weigh everything against the kid variable before you do it."

"Like moving here, to Morrisville."

"Oh, most definitely. I wanted a place where I could balance being a career woman and a mom, yet first and foremost it had to be a place where Bella could thrive. If she fails, no matter who I am or what greatness I achieve, it all amounts to nothing."

"A long-term investment," Bruce said, understanding.

"A child is very long-term. At least twenty years, if not more, before she's truly independent. I make so many decisions, but I won't know how any of them come out until years from now."

"Bella loves you a great deal," Bruce said.

"And sometimes I wonder why," Christina said. As soon as she'd said this, she also wondered why the words had slipped out—to Bruce, of all people. Maybe it was because he was an attentive listener who just naturally made a person trust him and want to share everything. Bruce was the type of lawyer who could get any smidgen of information out of his client.

Maybe it was the wide, engaging smile that cheekily promised all would be right in the world. Maybe it was the baby-blue eyes that had fathomless depths and that seemed able to read a woman's soul. Whatever it was, Bruce Lancaster was the type of man who made a woman want to fall for him. Bruce Lancaster was danger.

He reached across the table and covered her hand with his. The contact had been designed to reassure, to convey without words that he'd understood her fears as a mother. But his touch should be banned as a hazard. His fingers ignited something perilous. They made her feel, made her desire things that couldn't be.

"She loves you because you're her mother and you love her. It's unconditional."

"I know," Christina said. She jerked her hand back, freeing it from the magnetic enticement. Damn him for understanding, for being so, so…

She'd lost her train of thought; it had derailed somewhere in the muddled mess that was now her heart and her head. "I'm going to check on Bella."

"Don't," Bruce said firmly. "Don't run, Christina. Not from me. We may not have gotten off to a good start, but I'm not going to hurt you. Ever."

"This isn't proper," she said, remaining rooted to the cane chair.

"What's not proper?" he asked. "If my touching you in a show of understanding wasn't acceptable, then I apologize. We're working on a harassment case. I of all people understand the rules and don't intend to violate them."

But therein lay the problem. His advance, his touch, hadn't been unwanted. Hadn't been harassment at all. It had been wonderful. Sweet and caring. It had been the touch of a friend, and God knows she could use one of those. It had also hinted at a sexual chemistry, the promise of something deeper if she chose to let it.

It was something to think about. With Kyle she'd

been young, idealistic and in love with the idea of being in love. She'd clung to the ideal, deluded herself that all would be okay.

But Bruce's touch had done what Kyle never could have accomplished in a million years with a million dollars of fancy trinkets.

Bruce's touch had shown her equality: that Bruce saw her as a person in her own right, one with feelings that didn't require justification or rationalization. He saw her as someone real, not just an arm ornament to be taken out and played with on occasion.

His actions—mere friendship or those of courtship, whichever—had somehow hinted at normalcy. And she had to stop this encounter before it went any further. No longer would her normal depend on any man.

"I—" she began. "This is too fast for me."

"Too fast?" Bruce queried. He did not want to push her, but yet at the same time he had to know. He felt as if he'd been run over by an eighteen-wheeler. As much as he might desire Christina Jones, deep down he knew he shouldn't pursue her. For starters, he had to work with her. Yet he so wanted to investigate the feelings he was developing for her, to push and see where things could go.

"This is too fast. Us. Partners. Friends. Whatever is going on here that I can't put into words. I didn't even like you when I first met you, really met you, as a Lancaster and Morris lawyer—although I did have to agree with what the Brownie troop called you. Mr. Hunk. You are that."

He simply nodded and waited. He'd learned with

women that if you paused and gave the woman time, she'd tell you everything you wanted to know. Bruce wanted to know it all where Christina was concerned.

"I tried dating a bit after Kyle. It didn't work. No one interested me, and all I could think about was how I could be home with Bella doing something nurturing, something that would make her a better person, a strong female."

"There's nothing wrong with that."

"To my family there is. I should be remarried, preferably to someone Hispanic this time, and producing a horde of kids. Sure, I don't aspire to be single the rest of my life. But I've come to peace with my status. It's okay if I am single. I'm no longer afraid of being by myself. I brought Bella into the world."

Perplexed, Bruce frowned, but he remained silent.

"I can tell you don't understand. In life we pick paths. Robert Frost's 'The Road Not Taken' remains my favorite poem. Once you take a path, you can't go back, because time has marched on. As for marriage, I am not going to marry again just to avoid social stigma."

"So you'll turn down the right man?" That thought boggled and bothered him.

"No, but I'm not out there actively trying to find him. I'm no longer twenty and afraid of being alone. My priorities have changed. I'm probably not explaining this well, but as I've said before, my own happiness is secondary to that of the little girl in there. I will not have men in and out of my life, trying them on, searching for something that may not exist. Sure, someday I hope to be in a healthy relationship with a loving man, but until then, I can live without Mr. Right."

"So you'll sacrifice your own needs."

"Absolutely." The word burst forth with such firm conviction. "I would take a bullet for my daughter, and being single is easier than that. I've been on call 24/7 ever since the day I found out I was pregnant. Bella's birth didn't put a dent in Kyle's schedule. Hell, he wasn't even there. The game was too critical for him not to play."

"There has to be a compromise," Bruce said simply. "You say you want normal. Normal has to be somehow having it all."

"Bruce, not everyone is going to be happy and live the fairy tale. Period. I think that's a huge lie that someone somewhere made up to sell greeting cards or perfume. I think that there are people, like me, who catch snippets of true happiness here and there, but for the most part, we're simply to be content with what we have. Our purpose for being is for someone else. We aren't the ones playing the game. We're the coaches. Our satisfaction comes down the road later, when the choices we've made result in fruition."

"But you're not content, Christina," Bruce pointed out. "If you were, you would have stayed in Cincinnati and not moved to Morrisville."

"I didn't say that you had to settle for mediocrity and second best. I'm not living to grab my own brass ring, but to grab it for someone else. I don't have to have it for myself."

"Everyone needs it," Bruce said. "It's why I fight fires. There has to be that part of us that belongs only to us and no one else."

"Then mine is law," Christina said, the finality in her tone indicating any current introspection of her life and personality was over.

"Then let's get back to it," Bruce said. He fully opened the file folder. Not that his interest was anywhere on the page in front of him. He wanted to pick Christina's brain more, to see what made her tick. She more than fascinated him with her attitudes and opinions.

So far, all the women Bruce had met had been dying to get married. They'd been women on a mission, seeking that life partner for one reason or another. It could have been so that they'd belong somewhere—"I'm Mrs. So and So." Or it could have been so that they'd have access to someone else's money. Maybe some of it was love, but with all the women he'd met, Bruce didn't think that was really their motivation.

Except where Christina was concerned. He could see how much she loved her child. It was there in the way she sacrificed her own needs, in the way she got up and checked on Bella every fifteen minutes.

He and Christina stopped working around one, and lunch for everyone was chicken noodle soup and toast. Within minutes of lunch, Bella was once again asleep.

"She'll nap for a while," Christina said as she led the way back into the dining room. "Thank you for being so patient with her."

"Why wouldn't I be?" Bruce asked. That Christina

still thought the worst of him in some ways was becoming painfully obvious, and he resolved to change that immediately. "I like kids. I always wanted to grow up in a whole household of them. I was an only child so I was always over at the Morrises' house. Constant chaos. It was great. When I marry, I want kids."

"I grew up the middle child," Christina admitted. "It's a unique position."

"Tell me about your family," Bruce prodded. "I'd like to know."

"There's not much to tell. Both my siblings are very successful. Cecile is a pediatrician married to an internist. Two children, a dog and a nanny. Enrique runs the family business and has three children."

"And you're the lawyer," Bruce said.

"I'm the lawyer," Christina said. "And I went too far away to school—though Harvard is one of the best. They hated the idea of me working, so once they got over Kyle's being non-Hispanic, they were more than thrilled with my marrying him. Kyle Jones, football god."

A bemused smile crossed her face. "Though to hear them tell it now, they knew he was a cad from the start and I should have stuck to my own kind. That was after the lecture I got on how divorce should never be an option."

"Bella says you won't be going home for Thanksgiving."

"No, I'm not planning on it. It's a little too chummy and perfect. Overkill, you could call it. Besides, I have plans."

"Plans?" Bruce said, managing to keep his tone neutral. "Did Reginald Morris invite you to his place? It's standing knowledge that anyone who works at the firm or is a family friend can attend the Morris turkey day bash."

Christina shook her head. "Nope, nothing like that."

"Your plans aren't staying home alone, are they? Because that's not acceptable. Reginald refuses to let anyone be home alone. Thanksgiving is his big holiday. Even my grandfather will be there."

"Oh, I won't be alone. Far from it. Actually, it's good you brought Thanksgiving up. I'd like you to spend it with me."

Bruce eyed her suspiciously. The friendliness in Christina's tone was too forced. She'd never be good at poker; it was evident she was up to something. Although he did find himself wanting to spend the holiday with her.

"I usually go to the Morrises'," he said slowly.

"Not this year," Christina said. "Well, at least not at first. We have a dinner to attend."

That got his attention. "We do?"

"Why, yes," Christina replied, her expression guarded. "In fact, we're the hosts."

# Chapter Eight

They were hosting a dinner. Even a week after her announcement, he resisted the urge to pinch himself. She'd steamrolled him, which was pretty impressive. No one else had ever accomplished that.

Reginald had been supportive when he'd stopped by Bruce's office in the morning and said he'd be at the country club tomorrow. "It'll get me out of from under the wife's thumb before my own bash starts," he'd said.

Bruce himself had to admit the past week had been interesting. He'd spent Thursday and Friday at Christina's house. Then she'd been in the office on Monday and Tuesday, and they'd holed up in the conference room for hours on end. It was now Wednesday afternoon, and she was at the club, making the last of the arrangements for their dinner party.

Oh, yes, while the cat had been away at Cyntech, the mouse had been out proving that she wasn't afraid to play ball in the big leagues.

They were hosting a Thanksgiving dinner for all their class-action clients and their families.

He should be ticked off. Even though she was a senior partner, this was his case. Or that was what he'd
told her the first day. But to use the cliché, she'd
grabbed the bull by the horns and run. She'd just done
what she'd wanted to do.

And darn it, all the other work she'd done? Flawless.
He hadn't been able to make one complaint. Even the
idea of a dinner was exceptional. Maybe that was why
he'd simply mumbled "Great job" and kept his mouth
shut. Bruce was enough of a man to know when to quit.
If Christina had wanted to prove her competence, she
had—in spades.

He'd ignored the one knowing smirk she'd given
him that afternoon at her house, and that had been that.
A new partnership had been formed, somewhat precari-
ously perhaps, but a new understanding existed between them now that hadn't been there previously. No
longer was Bruce "in charge," and oddly, he found
himself not minding the cessation of control. Being
equal partners with someone worthy of you was a
pretty cool thing.

And Christina was a one-woman dynamo. She'd rescheduled with Elaine Gray and her legal team for December sixth, giving everyone the week between
Thanksgiving and the meeting to get prepared.

As for tomorrow, Bruce sighed. He was hosting a
Thanksgiving party, more specifically an early-
afternoon holiday feast with all the trimmings. With
Christina at his side. Once he'd gotten over his initial
shock, he'd thought of nothing else. He liked the idea

of being with her. Besides, he could still attend the Morris bash after all was said and done.

Bruce glanced at the clock. Everyone else had ditched work early. He might as well go home, too. Tomorrow would be an interesting day.

THANKSGIVING DAY dawned clear, bright and cold. Rumor had snow moving in later that evening, but the afternoon should remain partially sunny, according to the local weather forecaster.

Christina shrugged off her nervousness as she stepped out of bed. The dinner began at one-thirty, ensuring that anyone who had worked second shift the night before had had enough time to get a decent night's sleep. For some whose days and nights were backward, they would technically be having turkey for breakfast, but no one had seemed to mind or care. When Christina had invited María Gonzales, the woman's eyes had teared up. More than likely, turkey hadn't been on the day's menu at all for the Gonzales family.

But a dinner for all the members of their class-action suit and their families was only the first step. Christina had talked to local churches and businesses since the inception of her idea, and she'd managed to get a plethora of gift certificates donated. Every family would receive something that they could use to usher in the holiday season.

She herself was so fortunate; it was the least she could do. Now, if only she wasn't riding to the event with Bruce, she might just be able to calm down.

"So, ARE YOU READY?"

"I think so," Christina said. She nervously smoothed out a temporary crinkle in her black knit pants. Bruce stood in her foyer, waiting. Why she'd let him talk her into going with him was still a mystery. But his argument on the phone this morning had been so persuasive she'd caved. God forbid they ever be on opposing sides of a case.

Tonight's dress code called for casual, although Christina knew by saying that, that the women and their families would be dressed in Sunday best. Everyone would be scrubbed clean, clothes neatly pressed.

Christina herself wore simple black pants, a white broadcloth shirt with a stand-up collar, and a black knit vest with a ribboned gray cat face on one of two patch pockets. Her plain black pumps put her about three inches shorter than Bruce.

She had to admit her breath had caught in her throat for a second when she'd opened the door and let him in. He'd chosen to wear a dark-blue flannel shirt and tan chinos. The color combination sharpened his blue eyes and accentuated his dark-brown hair. He'd put on dress cowboy boots, the broken-in kind worn for two-stepping and church. All that was missing was a Stetson.

Sensing her current appraisal, Bruce let loose that grin of his and said, "So I'll do?"

"You're fine." Christina managed to regain her composure on the little white lie. He was more than fine, but she wouldn't stroke his ego with any additional compliments. The man already had all the sexual ammunition in the world to use against her; she wasn't going to hand him the gun, too, by letting him know he'd had an effect on her. "Let's go."

The parking lot was almost empty when they arrived. When she'd made the reservations, the country club's catering manager had told Christina that the club's annual Thanksgiving dinner began at five.

Christina pretty much assumed they'd be finished with their party before then. While she had no embarrassment about being seen with any of her guests, she didn't wish them to feel uncomfortable or inferior, or be subjected to any speculative glances should they run into any of Morrisville's elite. And all but two of the women would be there. They were both out of town visiting family.

"Stay there," Bruce ordered as he turned off the rumbling diesel engine. Within moments he'd come around and opened her door.

"You know, I've gotten out of this truck before by myself," Christina said.

He grinned. "Yeah, but then you were ticked at me."

A blast of cold air brushed by under her coat, and Christina reached for Bruce's hands. Warmth caused her fingers to tingle as Bruce helped her down. He placed a steadying hand on her lower back, a gentle pressure she felt through the heavy wool fabric. Then they hurried inside, where the banquet manager greeted them and led them to the banquet room.

"Flowers?" Bruce questioned, eyeing the table as they entered the room.

"Absolutely," Christina said. "They add a little glamour to any occasion, let people feel valued. Come here. I'll put yours on."

Although perhaps that was a mistake. Because in order to pin the boutonniere to his shirt, Bruce had to undo a few of the buttons. And then Christina had to slide her fingers under the soft flannel material, not even an inch from the skin of his chest.

Being tall and this close, she could also smell the aftershave he wore, a deep musky scent designed to weaken women at the knees. At least, it was having that effect on her. She trembled slightly and managed not to stab him with the long straight pin.

"Steady," Bruce said.

"I'm fine. See? Done. Now, please, if you don't mind, will you add mine? I could do it myself, but I always manage to get it crooked."

"Sure," Bruce said, but the thought temporarily paralyzed him. He stared at her. There was a reason that, in high school, he'd always bought his dance dates wrist corsages. Slide on, slide off. No pins.

He'd experienced womanly delights on many occasions, and he was not a fumbling boy any longer. But this was Christina, and being invited into her personal space, if only to attach a flower to her black vest, had him suddenly as quaky as a teenager.

"You have done this before?" she asked, concerned.

"Of course," he replied gruffly. Did she have to smell so great? It wasn't even her perfume, but her hair. The result created a raised awareness of her as a woman, and a desire to be more than just her coworker.

"Be careful," she said. "Firefighters don't injure people."

"It's been a while," he said, forcing control into his fingers as they fumbled with the large straight pin. He'd lifted the left side of her vest, the one above the cat face, and his fingers grazed the white material directly above her breast. He could feel the heat of her breath, sense the rhythmic thumping of her heart.

"Thank you," she said as he finished and stepped back, the white carnation perfectly positioned. Her brown eyes had darkened, but maybe that was a trick of the chandelier lights. Or perhaps she, too, had been experiencing desire, need.

"You're welcome," Bruce said. He was spared any other conversation or thoughts about how dangerous Christina was to his libido as the first of their guests began to arrive.

The dinner was an unequivocal success, and around 5:00 p.m. the last of the guests departed. Reginald Morris had come and gone, extending an invitation to Christina to stop by his house later that day.

"You pulled it off," Bruce said as the room emptied, even the banquet staff taking off for a quick break before they returned and did teardown. "Well done."

"Thanks," Christina said. "Aren't you glad you didn't say anything?"

Bruce grabbed his water goblet. They were seated at one of the round tables sprinkling the room. He feigned stupidity. "About what?"

Christina smirked, for she had him. "Ah, spoken like

a true legal mind. About the dinner. Admit you wanted to complain when you first heard about it. Come on. Be a man and confess it."

He arched an eyebrow and was rewarded with a blush. "Now, why would I want to do that?" he drawled. "Every lawyer knows how hard it is to retract a confession."

She pounced. "Ha. Just say that you didn't think it was a good idea. Because you didn't think I was competent enough to pull it off. Because I did it all without your permission."

"Well, if I did think those things—for which of course I'm not admitting any guilt—you certainly proved me wrong, didn't you? You were more than competent, and this was more than superb."

Christina's smile widened into something real. "Ah, music to my ears and all the thanks I needed today."

She was letting him off the hook this easily? "An easy-to-please woman? No way," Bruce joked. "Don't you have a plan to take my nose, rub it in some dirt or something?"

"You're a cad," Christina said. "I thought that the day I met you but decided not to stoop to your level."

A low blow, delivered with humor, but still one he definitely deserved. And because she hadn't delivered it with malice, he knew they'd again forged new ground, putting their tumultuous start behind them.

"Seriously, you did a great job today, Christina. I'm going to echo what Reginald said. Your gesture—this dinner—went a long way toward building these women's confidence and trust in us and our firm. And the gift certificates were a classy touch. This dinner was a great idea. I'm glad you didn't run it by me."

"I had to do it. Those women deserve so much more. America is supposed to be the land of opportunity, and they've had so little of it. Compared with them, I'm totally assimilated. I've got the brass ring already. Everyone deserves a break that doesn't reek of charity."

"And this dinner didn't. You done good, Christina," Bruce joked, deliberately using poor grammar. Then his expression sobered. "Even if it had been my idea, I couldn't have done better."

An awkward silence descended as each contemplated Bruce's admission. A few of the banquet staff wandered back into the room and began cleaning up. "Probably time to go," Christina said. She didn't want to contemplate this change of events further, didn't want to tread new ground that might be too dangerous to her independence.

"You're right about the time," Bruce agreed, "especially since we have to stop by the Morrises' Thanksgiving dinner. Although, truth be told, I doubt I could eat another bite."

"We're stopping by?" Her brown eyes widened. "I wanted to go straight home."

He shook his head and gave her a sympathetic glance. "You heard Reginald while he was here. He told you to come by. That means he expects to see you."

"You can't drop me off and make my excuses?" she asked.

"I can, but I won't. This is the biggest party of the year that the Morris family gives. Everyone in the firm drops by at one point or another, even if it's just for a few minutes on the way to somewhere else."

"Well, if it can be brief, I guess we can stop for a minute or two. Tonight I planned on spending a quiet evening in."

The party would give him more time to spend with her, and Bruce realized he wanted every one of those precious minutes. "You can be alone tomorrow," he insisted. "Have the day to yourself then. Tonight, humor me. Think of it as being good for your career."

"But if I asked you to take me home…?" Christina began.

"I would," Bruce admitted. She responded with a relieved smile. "But you aren't going to ask, because you are dying to find out where one of your bosses lives, and where your cantankerous partner spent most of his childhood hanging out."

"Now, how could I resist that offer?" Christina removed her carnation and set it on the table. She stood. "Come on, let's leave so that they can clean up. I'm sure they'd like to go home sometime tonight."

"You're not keeping that?"

She shook her head. "I used to press flowers, but later I realized that as long as I had the memory, I had what I needed. I've never been much of a pack rat."

"I see," Bruce said, and for some reason, as she strode off to retrieve her coat, he removed the pin from her carnation and pocketed the bloom.

FIFTEEN MINUTES LATER, Christina found herself warmly welcomed into the Morris household. Located on the outskirts of town, in the more affluent section, their three-story Victorian sat on three-quarters of an acre in the center of the block. "It's a century home," Bruce whispered as Reginald said hello, took their coats and set his guests loose. "Been in the family about that long, as well."

"The dining room is huge," Christina said, for it was. Even Kyle's palatial estate didn't have this much room dedicated to formal eating. The table had been set for sixteen, and that was without squeezing the fine china place settings together. The room itself was decorated with antiques and painted in autumn colors.

"Bruce, great to see you." A petite female slid up next to Bruce, and Christina watched as the woman gave him a warm hug. Whoever this was, Bruce knew her well.

"Anne Louise, how are you?" Bruce returned the hug, which required him to bend slightly.

"I'm great. Adam and I've been busy." She patted her stomach. "Number four's on the way."

"Congratulations!" Bruce said. "I'm thrilled for you. Am I finally going to be a godparent?"

"Maybe this time. Maybe next," she said with a twinkle in her green eyes. "Adam and I plan on having at least five. You really ought to get working on some of your own, you know. Speaking of which…" Anne Louise turned a pointed gaze in Christina's direction and then scolded Bruce with a, "You're being rude. Introduce us. This is…?"

"Anne Louise is Reginald's youngest," Bruce offered Christina by way of explanation. "Anne Louise, this is Christina Jones. She's the newest senior partner at Lancaster and Morris. She and I are working on the Title VII case together. Christina, this is Anne Louise."

"Oh."

Christina sensed Anne Louise's momentary disappointment, as if she'd been hoping Bruce had brought a date. Then Anne Louise brightened. "Too bad, Bruce. We all keep believing you'll find someone. Anyway, welcome, Christina. Don't mind how cavalier all of us are regarding Bruce. I've known him practically since toddlerville. His parents live only a few houses down when they aren't traveling the world. It's a pleasure to meet you and put a name to the face of the newest senior partner. I'm Anne Louise Schuster, a nonlawyer, stay-at-home mom of three. My husband's into politics."

"So now you turn all bashful after you embarrass me? He's Indiana's junior senator," Bruce added. "Elected the moment he turned thirty-one. Anne Louise has to relocate her family to Washington, D.C., for part of each year."

"Which is ironic, considering I'm such a homebody. That and the fact that Adam and my father aren't in the same political party anymore," Anne Louise said with a laugh. "Dad got angry last election and cast a straight party ticket for the other side. Adam won his seat anyway."

"Speaking of which, is your husband around here somewhere?"

"Of course. He's in the family room, watching whatever sporting events happen to be on. This is his day to relax with the guys. Colin's back there, as are the rest of my brothers-in-law. Come on, Christina. Let me introduce you to all the womenfolk so that Bruce can go hang out with the guys. You'll quickly discover that there's a very sexist dividing line in this house and that we like it that way. Keeps the men out of our hair and our conversation. Can't talk about them if they're in the room. Would you like a glass of wine?"

"That sounds fine," Christina said, marveling at the friendly atmosphere of the Morris household. Things in Christina's house were much more formal, even at holidays. Here everything seemed so relaxed. As Bruce left them, a few children ran underfoot, and quickly Anne Louise hollered at them to go back down to the basement.

"We have beverages besides wine if you'd prefer something else," Anne Louise said as she also shooed a second group of kids downstairs. "Can you tell I'm craving a glass? Another nine months without. No hot-tubbing, no wine—remind me why do women do this again?"

"The result is worth it?"

"You mean controlled chaos?"

"That, too," Christina replied with a chuckle as she followed Anne Louise into the humongous kitchen that could only be described as a chef's dream. The original house had been expanded and the kitchen was modern and bright. Mrs. Morris had two Sub-zero side-by-side refrigerators, two sets of double ovens and a huge oversize center island workstation that could easily seat six. The room had to be thirty by forty, and included a large kitchen table, at which sat talking a multitude of women.

"You should see Mom's pantry," Anne Louise confided as she reached for an open bottle of wine from a countertop located away from the main workstation. "It's the size of a small bedroom. With four of us, Bruce and all our friends hanging out here, I think my mom fed the equivalent of a small army on a daily basis."

"Bruce did say he was always here," Christina remarked as she accepted the glass of Riesling that Anne Louise poured.

"He was. He and Colin—my brother, who works at Lancaster and Morris, too—he and Colin have been best friends simply for forever. They even roomed together all through college and law school. Between you and me, I think that Bruce was always happier being over here. His parents never really did recover after his sister's death. They never tried to have children again."

"He had a sister?" The news rocked Christina. Bruce had said he'd grown up an only child, and the death of any child was always terrible, no matter whose family.

"She died of SIDS at four months. Right before Halloween. He was four then, so I'm sure it remains one of his memories. His parents treated him as though he was fragile after that."

"Oh, my," Christina said.

"Exactly," Anne Louise said. "I have three, and I lived with the baby monitor next to my ear every night for months after they were born." She rubbed her stomach again. "I'm sure I will with this one, as well. She's due in June."

"I did pretty much the same thing. I have a daughter. Bella's eight now, but when she was little I would get up in the middle of the night and hold a mirror over her face to make sure she was breathing."

"Our children are our lives," Anne Louise said. "And that's my eldest, snagging carrot sticks. Good grief. He's growing like a weed."

Christina smiled and clutched her wineglass like a lifeline.

"Feel free to wander around," Anne Louise said. "Don't let me keep you cornered in here. The house is open—meaning, everyone is everywhere. Don't hesitate to give yourself a tour. There's a game room in the basement, and we have a rumpus room upstairs on the third floor. Just introduce yourself. I'd name everyone at that kitchen table over there for you, but it would take too long. Don't worry, no one bites."

"Except maybe me. If you'd like, I'll show you around." Bruce's voice tickled her ear, making Christina jump. A bit of wine sloshed out of her glass.

"Bruce," Anne Louise scolded. "Don't scare the poor girl. Look what you made her do. Now, go get a paper towel and clean this mess up."

"Yes, ma'am," Bruce said, retrieving a handful of paper towels from the holder next to the bar sink. He bent down and made a few easy swipes. When he straightened, the marble tile was dry. "Good as new."

"You're such a menace," Anne Louise said as Bruce

wadded up the towels and made the shot into the waste-basket. "Always have been."

"And I always will be, since I aim to please. So I'll take Christina on that tour before you start making her cook."

"Nah, we have this down to a system," Anne Louise said.

"The carrots, Anne Louise," a woman wearing an I'm the Cook apron called.

"I'm on it, Mom. I'm talking to Christina. She's the new senior partner who works with Dad."

"Hello, Christina," Mrs. Morris said.

"Hello," Christina greeted her.

"Hey, Bruce, are you two sitting at the head table?" one of Colin's sisters shouted.

"We ate at the club less than two hours ago," Bruce said. "Assign our spots to someone else."

"Oh, yes, the dinner," Mrs. Morris said, glancing up for a moment from whatever she was doing. "Reggie told me about that. How did it go?"

"Wonderful," Bruce answered as he led Christina out the kitchen door, Mrs. Morris's attention already diverted by the buzzing oven timer. "Overwhelmed yet?" Bruce asked as he guided Christina down a side hall that led by a half bath, the pantry and a set of back stairs.

"A little," she admitted. "And to think I was going to curl up with a good book and enjoy an evening of silence."

"Ah, sarcasm. I was starting to worry you'd lost your touch."

"I never lose my touch."

"That's good to know." Bruce cupped her elbow and drew her aside for a moment. And then totally blanked.

"Yes?" Christina prodded.

Bruce stared at her. Just what had he been about to say? Even in a courtroom he was always ready with a comeback, the next argument. He was never speechless. But the thought of her touch… "Uh."

She arched a blond eyebrow at him. "Cat got your tongue?"

As her mouth moved, he wished she had his tongue, in her mouth. He let go of her elbow, and some sanity returned. "Something like that. It's been a busy day."

"Have some wine. The few sips I've had of it seemed to help me."

He peered into her face. "Already had a beer. One's my limit. I'm driving, remember?"

Driving had never stopped Kyle. Another difference between the two men became glaringly obvious. Christina decided to stop comparing them. Bruce was by far the hands-down winner, and a complication she didn't need at this point. The last thing they should do was to give in to the undercurrent humming between them.

But right now, in the tiny hallway, how she wanted to give in! She'd leaned back against the wall, and Bruce moved close. All she had to do was reach up her hands and draw down his face to hers, press her lips to his. Her fingers itched to do just that, and she saw Bruce's expression darken.

He felt it, too.

"Oh, Bruce, there you are. Been trying to find you."

An elderly man dressed in a tweed sport coat and black slacks stood into the hallway, his expression revealing nothing. Christina froze. This situation was not what it seemed. It was not—

"I see you brought a date."

## Chapter Nine

At his grandfather's words, Bruce inwardly groaned. Christina had been about to kiss him, or at least she'd wanted to. And he'd wanted her to, even if she wasn't officially his date.

The interruption was as needed as a cold shower, and equally as unwelcome. Now Bruce remembered what he'd meant to tell Christina. Roy Lancaster, the old curmudgeon himself, was here, and wanting to meet her.

Bruce had simply forgotten it until too late.

"Granddad," Bruce said quickly, "this is Christina Jones, my new senior partner."

Roy's face, long able to school itself into any lawyerly facade, didn't show any surprise or shock. His blue eyes crinkled as he assessed Christina, and Bruce watched her shift uncomfortably. Heck, if Bruce hadn't grown up around Roy, he'd be unsettled, too. The man was a steamroller.

"Ah, so you're the new partner I've been trying to

meet for most of the month. Every time I drop by the office, you aren't there."

"We've been working from her house," Bruce said, his tone imploring Christina to keep silent. Her eyes widened with understanding. While Bruce knew she was strong enough to handle his grandfather, doing so was like cleaning your house—it was nicer when someone else did it for you.

"We've also been out in the field quite a bit," Bruce added. "We're getting ready for our December sixth meeting with the Morrisville Garment Company. Unless they surprise us and capitulate, we aren't hopeful for resolution. Afterward, if none is reached, we expect the EEOC to issue us the right-to-sue letter we've already asked for."

His grandfather's expression revealed he wasn't very interested in that piece of news. "I heard you held a party."

"We did," Bruce said, relieved that Christina was letting him handle this so far. "It was Christina's wonderful idea. It went a long way in building trust with our clients and showing them that the firm of Lancaster and Morris not only values them, but also respects them. That they aren't just an income source."

"And I charged it to my budget," Christina added.

As she said those words, Bruce winced. Roy Lancaster was the type who, in the courtroom, could make rabbits magically pop out of hats just when all had been said and done and the trial was wrapping up. Now his gaze had sharpened into that razor expression that meant he was far from finished here.

"Christina, I read your résumé. Refresh my memory. You went to Harvard, correct?"

"Yes, sir," Christina replied, her use of the title not lost on Bruce.

"Tell me, is my old friend Andy Buchanan still teaching there?"

"I had him my freshman year and then he retired."

"Ah," Roy said, as if mulling that fact over. "Did he ever talk about our case?"

Bruce willed Christina to be quiet, but she fell for Roy's trap. "Your case?" she asked.

"Yes, the one I beat him on. *Wedlock* v. *Storm.* Even though he lost badly, we kept in touch afterward for many, many years. Come, I want to hear your opinion on it, and then you can comment on the cases the Supreme Court recently announced it wouldn't hear."

"Like *Durnin* v. *Tower.*"

"Especially that one. My personal opinion is that some new, younger judges should be infused into the lower courts. Except that sometimes they aren't yet savvy in all the intricacies of the law."

"So did you or didn't you vote for Adam Schuster's political party?" Bruce asked, trying to wave the red cape in front of the charging bull that was his grandfather. "They ran on a platform of family values and more conservative judges, even if they are younger."

"Of course I voted for Adam's party. The party Reggie voted for would have fleeced my social security benefits. Come, Christina, let's find somewhere quieter."

Christina gave Bruce a glance and he shrugged as

Roy began leading Christina out of the hall. At least Bruce had tried. "Would it surprise you, Christina, that I told Reginald his son-in-law could end up president? I wonder if he's got something to hide should the secret service start snooping around."

"I doubt that's it," Christina said.

"I wouldn't," Roy said matter-of-factly.

Bruce watched Christina disappear. "Going to save her won't help," a voice behind him said.

"Yeah, I know," he said as Anne Louise approached. "She'll have to battle Roy on her own. He'll either love her or hate her."

"The old curmudgeon," she said. "You should have seen him at Adam's victory party. You would have thought he'd single-handedly gotten Adam elected."

"I'm sure in his mind he did," Bruce admitted with a smile. He could just picture his grandfather holding court and waving his drink. "It's got to be hard to be seventy and facing mortality, although everyone says Roy's just too mean ever to die."

"He's correct about the judges, though," Anne Louise said. "Adam says the same thing. Some of them are there way past their time."

"Yeah, but we'll never see a constitutional amendment eliminating judge tenure any more than we would see one setting a minimum age for being a federal judge."

"You know, you'd make a good judge someday," Anne Louise said.

"You think?" Bruce said. He shook his head. "Nope. Politics isn't for me. I refuse to enter those rat-race elections for county circuit court. And I haven't been practicing for a full ten years yet to qualify for anything higher."

"That's the county and state level. As you said, there are no minimum ages for federal judgeships," Anne Louise pointed out. "Wouldn't Roy just love for you to be a Supreme Court justice someday? Maybe once Adam's in there long enough he can pull some strings and get you a federal spot."

"Yeah, if he's president of the United States, like Roy said. Until then, I doubt our current president knows who I am, much less knows me well enough to think about appointing me," Bruce said.

"You never know," she said.

Bruce gave Anne Louise a quick kiss on the forehead. "Okay, I can't stand it. I have to go check on Christina."

AFTER FIFTEEN MINUTES, Christina had to admit she'd never met anyone quite like Roy Lancaster. For one, he was a thinner version of Colonel Sanders. Add a white suit with a black tie, and Roy Lancaster could easily grace a red-and-white-striped bucket of chicken.

She'd already guessed that the refilled cocktail now in his hand was more for show; that while everyone may have assumed he'd had "one too many," she'd noticed that the codger really had been sipping very, very slowly and that the drink appeared watered down.

He wasn't nearly as inebriated as everyone thought. He'd simply mastered the art of the show.

No wonder he'd been such a legal wizard. Once he'd

gotten her into a small study, he'd patted a wing chair on one side of the fireplace. He'd sat across from her, the gas logs in the fireplace providing mock cheer. After starting their conversation with the admission that he hadn't been too keen on her being hired in the first place—his honesty a tactic to throw her, she was certain—Roy drilled Christina rapid fire.

Five minutes into the interrogation, for that was all she could assume it was, a grudging respect loosened the taut lines around his mouth. A new light shone in his blue eyes, and he reached over, patted her hand and said simply, "You'll do."

Christina figured that whatever the test, she'd passed. Maybe not with flying colors, but passed nonetheless. For now, that would be good enough. She'd pitted her legal mind against Roy's, and that had been tough. She didn't want a repeat, and she'd never play him in chess, either.

"Here you are," Bruce said. He carried a fresh glass of wine, Christina noticed. Clever man. "I figured you might like a refill."

"Didn't have to come rescue her, boy. There's no emergency here," Roy said, seeing through the ruse.

"Besides discussing some court cases, your grandfather and I have been talking about the future of the firm," Christina said as she accepted the red wine. She'd left her previous glass somewhere in the kitchen after the spill. "He said I'd do."

"And she will, too," Roy averred, his blue eyes blazing. "Darn fine lawyer she'll make. You could do a lot worse. In fact, you often have."

"She's not—"

"Didn't say she was," Roy said sharply, and Christina bit her lip to hide her amusement at the exchange. "Just said at least you'd be associating with a higher class of female this time. Don't want any bimbos at Lancaster and Morris."

"Or in the lineage," Bruce said dryly.

"That, too," Roy acknowledged with an exaggerated huff. "Took your mother a bit to win me over once she married my son. And speaking of her, she hasn't been too pleased with any of your choices to date, either."

"When it's time, I'll know," Bruce said. "Like golf. The season's over. In fact—" his brow creased "—it's snowing."

"We're supposed to get a dusting," Anne Louise said, entering the room. Christina wondered if everyone had felt the urge to save her, until Anne Louise announced, "Dinner's almost ready. Time to take your places. Come on, Grandpa Roy. We can't start without you in your traditional place."

"Darn right," he said.

As Roy rose to his feet, Christina followed Bruce's glance out the window. "That's not a dusting," she said. "Those flakes are huge."

"And wet," Bruce replied. He pulled out his cell phone. "I'd better call in and see what's going on. Usually, at times like this everyone's needed."

"Firefighting," Roy announced for Christina's benefit. "I told you I served on the department, didn't I?"

"If you didn't, I can assure you that Bruce told me," she said. "Family tradition."

"And we're big on tradition around here," Roy announced. "Not that we're stick-in-the-muds."

"Never," Anne Louise said. "Grandpa Roy. Dinner. You're seated where you like to be, at the end next to my mother."

"Did she make the cranberry sauce herself? No canned stuff for me," Roy declared to no one in particular. He wobbled for a moment as he took a step. Christina wanted to laugh. What a player. Roy was now leaning on Anne Louise for support, even though he'd been fine to walk in with Christina. They didn't make them like Roy anymore.

"Of course it's homemade cranberry sauce," Anne Louise replied. "My mother doesn't allow anything canned in her kitchen unless it's out of season and she's desperate."

With that they departed, leaving Bruce and Christina alone in the small study. Christina rose and moved to the window. Even in the darkness, it was easy to see that the snow was heavy, and falling fast. Already a quarter to a half inch had deposited itself on the roads, lawns and roofs.

Bruce snapped his cell phone shut, and Christina turned around. "Some dusting," he said. "We have way too much moisture in the air. They're predicting anywhere from one to two feet."

"One to two feet?" Having gone to college in Boston, Christina was no stranger to snow, but two feet was a lot.

"Yeah, it's a fast-moving storm. Like the one we had in December 2004. Dumped one to two feet all the way from southern Missouri to Lake Erie in a very short time frame. St. Louis and Chicago saw nothing, while Kentucky had every major highway closed. Even places as far south as Houston saw snow—for many, the first in decades. You're about to have that quiet night after all, because I'd better get you home before the roads get bad. Even though the fire department said they don't require my services right now, I have a feeling I'll be paged in later. A lot of people are going to get stuck in this."

"Okay," she said. She reached for the glass of wine so she could return it to the kitchen.

"My grandfather wasn't too hard on you?" Bruce asked as they walked.

For Bruce to worry about her was sweet, and his concern touched her. "I can see what made him such a good courtroom litigator, that's for sure. He's still pretty sharp."

"He was one of the great orators of his time. The man modeled himself after Abe Lincoln. Be a self-made man and keep it short and concise. He cites the 'Gettysburg Address' as the best speech ever written. Here, I'll take that."

Now in the kitchen, Bruce emptied the contents of her glass into the sink and set the goblet on the countertop. "Our coats are probably upstairs. If you wait here, I'll go for them."

"Okay," Christina said, using the moment to survey the cavernous kitchen, now empty of adults. Only a rowdy group of children sat at the kitchen table. Their ages ranged from four to about eleven, and all were happily stuffing their faces with food. The two older boys were arguing about which game system was best—Nintendo or Playstation—each boy's voice getting louder as he argued his case. They were lawyers in the making.

Bella would have loved celebrating Thanksgiving here, Christina mused. Although Kyle's family treated Bella like a princess, since she was around all adults, Bella was to be seen and not heard. She would have enjoyed playing with the other kids in such an informal environment, especially with all the girls, who appeared to be about Bella's age. And while Christina hadn't toured the finished basement or third-floor playroom, she had a feeling that they would be kid-friendly spaces akin to heaven.

"You seem down," Bruce said as he returned with her wool coat. "Is everything okay?"

"I'm just missing Bella," Christina answered. "She's probably in her best party dress at a be-seen-but-not-heard party at Kyle's parents' house. Her only cousin is still eight months old, so she has no one to play with."

"Next year if she's spending the holidays with you, you'll have to bring her here. Reginald and Loretta will insist."

"I can't plan that far," Christina said. "I'm still renting my house and taking things one day at a time."

"Come on, we'll talk at your place. Let's begin making our way to the door. While I was upstairs, I used the truck's remote start, so by the time we're finished with the goodbyes, the truck should be warmed up. If not, both front seats have heaters. I'm man enough to admit that I turn them on."

Twenty minutes later, Christina was glad for those seat warmers. The temperature had dropped and snow was thicker still, having blanketed everything in sight with more than an inch of snow already. Most of Morrisville was relatively flat and the roads straight, and the large four-wheel-drive truck handled the snowy trek with ease.

Bruce pulled up into her driveway and again assisted with her exit. She managed that fine, but her black pumps were little match for the snow, and she slipped on her walkway.

"Steady. I've got you," he said, cradling her safely against his broad chest. Snow touched her face and melted on her nose and lips. "Looks like it's getting even heavier. Let's get you inside. The last thing you need is to catch cold."

A thought struck her, and Christina turned around. "All those people at the Morrises'—they were just sitting down for dinner."

"Oh, most of them will stay for the night, including my grandfather. He'll hold court until at least ten. The rest live close enough to walk home if necessary. Loretta's known for keeping a box of extra hats and gloves for emergencies like tonight's."

Christina had left the front light on, and the roofed

porch provided a brief respite from the falling snow. She rummaged in her purse for her key, and at last lugged out the oversize photo key chain Bella had made for her at a children's museum. "You'd think that the size of this thing would make it easier to find," she said, her fingers shaking, and not only from the cold.

Why was she nervous? Bruce wasn't going to consider her incompetent because she'd taken a few extra seconds to find her keys.

There was no way she was nervous just because Bruce had held her close for a moment to keep her from landing in the snow. He'd have done that for anyone. This wasn't a date. But he *had* almost kissed her in the hallway. She pushed that evidence aside. They were simply two work partners who'd gone to a work function together. That was all.

He stamped his right foot on the porch and retrieved the key chain from her fumbling fingers. "Here, let me," he said. His warm cloud of breath touched her cheek.

Bruce unlocked the door and held it open for her, letting her step inside first. He shut the door quickly and handed her back her keys. She dumped them in her purse, which Bruce removed from her hands. "You're freezing. Let's get those shoes off. They've got snow in them, which will only melt and make your feet wet."

"I guess that's one benefit of wearing cowboy boots," she said as Bruce leaned down and grabbed her ankle. She stilled and he lifted her foot. His touch felt solid through her thin hose.

"Yeah, these boots are oiled enough to make them

waterproof. A good pair of cowboy boots lasts forever." He removed one shoe, then did the same with other. "To the family room. I'm not leaving until you're warmed up."

"Really, I'm okay," Christina said. "This is not necessary."

"Yes, it is. Bella was just sick, and I am not letting you become ill and miss the meeting with the Grays."

"Like that would happen. I'm too tough," Christina said, but already he was leading her into the family room, guiding her onto the couch. As soon as she sat, she realized how tired she was. Even the bright lights weren't enough to keep her from yawning. And was Bruce now sitting next to her, rubbing her stocking-clad feet?

"See, even tough girls can use a little TLC," Bruce said, continuing his wonderful ministrations. "We ate early this afternoon. What are you going to eat later? You must stay nourished."

"Some soup," Christina said, closing her eyes. Opening cans with pop tops was simple. She concentrated on how heavenly her feet felt. The man was a god. The way his fingers worked magic against the arch and balls of her feet should be bottled. She'd make a fortune if she could sell what he was doing to her instep to the highest bidder....

He could continue this all night and she'd let him. Too bad his cell phone was beeping.

She focused her eyes slowly, her pupils again getting used to the white light that flooded her family room. The hands that had been on her feet were now checking a cell phone.

"Lousy timing," Bruce said, and Christina couldn't agree more. Bruce held the phone to his ear, removing it once he'd heard the message.

It was probably best that the foot rub was over, especially since she didn't know where it would have stopped. The call had saved her from making the choices, yet Christina didn't find she was grateful. "What is it?"

"There's a three-car pileup on a highway exit ramp. I've got to go. Tell you what. How about you make me a late lunch tomorrow and I'll do your sidewalk and driveway."

"You'll shovel my driveway?"

That Dennis Quaid grin widened wickedly. "Didn't say I was going to shovel. I have a snow blower. A real man's machine, too, not one of the wimpy ones that barely cuts a path. Besides, we have some conversations to finish."

She had to admit she was confused. "We do?"

"We do," Bruce said. He moved into her proximity and leaned down. His face loomed and Christina's lips parted slightly. Was he going to kiss her? And would she mind? Should she stop him?

But his mouth pressed her forehead, instead, although the touch of his lips to her skin was not chaste or brotherly. It left her craving more.

She couldn't read his expression, only recognize the roughness in his voice as he said, "If that's unwanted, you can slug me and sue me tomorrow. See you around one. We'll talk then."

"One o'clock," Christina echoed, watching him stride across the floor and leave the room. Within moments she heard her front door slam and the reassuring rumble of the big diesel truck as it drove off into the night. Only then did she rise and go dead-bolt the front door.

But his being there couldn't be locked out, at least not in her mind. He'd rubbed her feet, and her body had wanted him to inch his hands higher, over her calves, then up over her thighs. He'd kissed her on the forehead, and sure the kiss had been quick, but it had contained something tender, like the softest touch of a rose.

Yes, she'd wanted more.

Darn, but the man had an effect on her. Christina shook herself, trying to eradicate the chill that now stole over her. What would have happened had he not been paged?

Could she have resisted him? Or would he have swept her away, with her a willing and happy participant in her own demise?

Chemistry was a powerful thing. As Christina stood at the window and watched the snow fill in Bruce's footsteps, another realization dawned. The snow was a beautiful paradox—harmless and gorgeous on her lawn, while at the same time dangerous to those in that auto accident on the exit ramp.

Just as the man who'd left was a paradox. Seemingly harmless, but oh, so delightfully dangerous. He made her question her existence. Made her wonder if she could have it all, or if she'd find herself left out in the cold again, holding nothing.

And that remained to be seen.

## Chapter Ten

Bruce arrived promptly at one. Christina had found herself restless most of the night, lying awake in her bed, trying to understand the disturbing effect he had on her. She had also missed Bella's presence, and had taken little comfort in the fact that she'd talked to her daughter first thing this morning around eight. Bella had complained about not feeling well, but Kyle's mother had assured Christina that it was nothing that a little pediatric cold medicine wouldn't fix.

Christina's maternal radar was zinging, but there was nothing she could do. She'd brought most of the case files home, and even rereading them hadn't relieved an internal sense of dread that something was wrong.

Perhaps it was that Bruce was coming, and very politely she'd have to tell him that whatever this sexual undercurrent was between them, it would just have to remain unexplored. Oh, she'd admitted to herself in the wee hours of the night that she'd like to explore it, but the list of reasons for not proceeding far outweighed any temporary pleasure being in his arms might provide.

But how to tell him? That was the question plaguing her. He'd said they'd talk, so she was sure he was prepared for her reaction and would take it like the good sport he was. He had to be a good sport; he was already plowing her driveway. He hadn't even knocked, just started the task the moment he'd arrived and exited his truck.

The machine was the beast he'd described it as, and the path it cleared was impressive. He'd already cut a sizable swath in the driveway and had almost reached the detached garage's double door.

She let the sheer lace curtain drop back into place. She'd opened three cans of vegetable soup, dumped them in a pot and now had everything simmering on the stove. She'd whipped together some quick drop biscuits, and those were ready to go into the oven the moment he began the sidewalk. She had hot chocolate ready in a Thermos, and she'd found herself so tense this morning she'd baked a made-from-scratch chocolate cake.

She chided herself one last time. She wasn't breaking up with him. He hadn't even asked her out. They'd never kissed. She was a grown woman. But a part of her longed for Bruce, the part he'd stirred when he'd reminded her that she had needs. She craved that "normal."

Still, having it all was an illusion and normal was a myth, as much as she'd love to convince herself otherwise. She'd learned the truth with Kyle.

Hearing the snow blower cease, she knew Bruce would be soon stomping on her back porch, kicking the snow off his heavy snow boots. She pictured him in her mind as he brushed the snow off his parka and snow pants, saw him enter her laundry room and strip the garments off his body.

And then there he was, standing in her kitchen. Her throat constricted and her mouth dried. Even wearing wool socks, the man was desirable. Could those blue jeans get any tighter, and the navy long-sleeved Morrisville Fire Department shirt reveal more-honed chest muscles?

How could she be so crazy to think of letting him go and denying their chemistry? Any woman would want this man to walk into her kitchen, especially with the warm smile meant just for her.

"Something smells really good," Bruce said as he padded over. He lifted the pot lid. "Mmm. Vegetable soup. One of my favorites."

"I don't usually eat meat," Christina said. Kyle had thought that a tad freakish, but Bruce took it in stride.

"Nothing wrong with that. Vegetables are fine by me. I happen to like them," Bruce replaced the lid. "And hot soup sounds perfect for someone who's been clearing snow."

"The biscuits should be done in a few minutes," she said.

He leaned a little closer. "You made biscuits?"

"From a mix, but yes. The cake for dessert is home-made, though."

"You're going to spoil me."

She'd love to spoil him. "It was nothing," she said instead.

"So did you eat last night?"

"No," she admitted under his watchful gaze. "I went to bed early. How did your call go?"

"No one was hurt. One of the cars is probably totaled, but the driver and his passenger walked away without injury. They got lucky."

"I couldn't believe we ended up with eighteen inches of snow," Christina said. "Some dusting."

"And it should all hang around until Sunday. When Bella comes home she can build a snowman or something." He saw her face cloud. "What is it?"

"She said she wasn't feeling well. Even though my ex-mother-in-law swears it's nothing, I'm still worried."

"That's natural," Bruce said. The timer dinged. "Biscuits?"

"Biscuits." Christina confirmed. "Do you mind eating in here?"

"Not at all. Let me wash up first."

When he planted himself at her kitchen table a few minutes later, she wondered if she should have suggested eating in the dining room. The table would have been larger, and she would have been able to sit without her knees accidentally touching his.

"Thank you for doing my sidewalks," she said, deciding to start on a safe topic.

"You're welcome," he replied.

Christina stirred her soup with her spoon. "You're not making this easy."

He paused, a steaming bite of biscuit mere inches from his lips. "What do you mean?"

"This. We're law partners. And you're clearing my driveway and I'm feeding you soup and biscuits and my legs keep getting caught in yours."

"There's something wrong with that? This is a small table and you do have nice legs."

"Oh, you know it's more than this. You're driving me crazy. I can't figure out which end is up. Maybe you should hit on me. Get it over with."

"Hit *on* you? Like a punch on the face? A blow to your knee? Can't do it. My mother raised me to be a gentleman. Don't hit ladies."

He knew exactly what she'd meant, but the lawyer in him had shredded her point just to be ornery. "You are so infuriating," she said.

"It's part of my charm." His face suddenly lost its playfulness. "Seriously, though, I sense you have something to say, and that's what we said today was about. I'll cut to the chase for you. Not going to happen."

"What? Talk?"

"No. We're about to do that."

She settled back into her chair, relief mingling with confusion. Bruce scared her, but not in the traditional sense. He made her want to break down the barriers that she'd erected to protect herself. She wanted to hang up her boxing gloves, though she believed that wasn't possible. "So since it's not going to happen, you'll back off and let me and whatever this sexual connection is be?"

"No." His penetrating gaze held hers. "That's what's *not* going to happen."

Her brow creased, and as she opened her mouth, his forefinger inched up, indicating he wanted her to shush.

"Christina, this isn't romantic, and I apologize for that. But someone has to take control here. I'll move slow, but you must understand something. This—us— is something that I believe we must pursue."

Her jaw dropped. "What? We've known each other a little over a month."

He set his spoon back in the bowl and leaned toward her. "Exactly. And our relationship has been like opening a Pandora's box. I've thought of little else since I first stepped into this house a few weeks ago. I want to know why you're under my skin. Why you affect me so much. Why you're so wrong for me, and why you're so right. Why I never thought I'd fall for a woman who'd been married once, but why now I can't imagine falling for anyone else. I want you, Christina. You can't deny a man for trying for more, especially where you are concerned. When I play, I play for keeps. And let me reassure you, with you, you-me-us is not a game. I've meant every word I've said."

She simply stared at him. His hand was now covering hers, its heat infusing hers with much-needed—and much-dreaded—warmth. To let the charm of Bruce Lancaster sweep her away would be so simple. Yet she'd let herself be swept away before—with disastrous results. That Bruce was totally different from Kyle, that he treated her like an equal partner, didn't matter. The fear of the unknown, of failing and floundering, froze her. "I...I can't," she finally stammered.

"I know." His expression was full of understanding, which didn't make the situation easier. If he'd been angry, she could have put on those proverbial boxing gloves, flail on him and send him down and out.

"I understand, Christina. 'It's too soon,' 'Not the best time,' 'Bella,' and a million of other excuses that help you keep that protective wall solid and safe around your heart. You've risked so much that if we tried, and got it all wrong, everything you've worked for and built would wash away like wood in a flooded creek. I know, Christina. Believe me, I know."

"I'm sorry," she said, for what else was there to say? Were she a character on a soap opera, at this moment more than a million women would be yelling at the television, screaming how stupid she was.

But they didn't walk in her shoes. They didn't understand. When you started over, you had to stand alone. You had to save yourself. Until she truly succeeded at that, whether a month from now or years from now, she wasn't free to share her life again.

Life was a game you couldn't cheat at.

"So what do we do now?" she finally asked.

"Nothing," Bruce said with a shrug. He'd been toying with her fingers. Abruptly, he dropped them and moved his hand back to his soupspoon. "We go on. We win this case. We become the best lawyers the state of Indiana has ever seen."

She gave him a tentative smile. "Friends?"

"Friends," Bruce parroted, though the word tasted flat. But he kept his disappointment well hidden from

Christina. He'd crossed the line when he'd kissed her forehead the previous night. But he'd needed something. Anything.

She wanted to be friends. Ha!

How many times had he told a woman, "We'll be friends"? They'd always smiled like a kicked puppy and bravely agreed. Then neither would call the other and that would be that. Only one woman had told him directly, "We'll never be friends. Let's not even pretend." Then she'd walked away, refusing even to glance back over her shoulder.

Being "just friends" with Christina was impossible. But if he rejected her offer, he'd close the door. So he'd be her friend, taking that to start with and ending up as lovers.

She wouldn't be privy to his intentions yet, though. He'd answered "nothing," but he hadn't said, *We do nothing.* For Bruce planned on doing something, and even though lawyers had to share all their discovery information with the opposing counsel, that didn't mean they didn't hide a few surprises up their sleeves.

The two of them finished their lunch in silence, each to his or her thoughts. "So, friend," he said after they'd cleared away the dishes, "how about you show me some of Bella's baby pictures and some family snapshots so I don't feel like an idiot if they ever visit and I'm here?"

She seemed surprised. "You'd like to see those?"

"Yeah." Anything giving him more insight into who she was and where she'd come from was more than welcome. He wanted to know everything about her.

Perhaps it might also break some of the ice around her heart, help her let him into her life.

"They're upstairs. Wait here and I'll get them."

"I'll finish cleaning up," he offered. As he was putting leftovers in, the phone rang. By the third ring it was obvious Christina either hadn't heard it or she couldn't reach it in time.

"Grab that," he suddenly heard her call, and Bruce snagged up the cordless receiver and pressed talk. "Jones residence."

"Who the hell is this?" a male voice growled into the receiver.

"Ms. Jones's answering service," Bruce said smoothly, although he was already more than a bit irked at the caller. He had a strong premonition who it was. "May I please tell her who's calling?"

"Yeah, this is her ex-husband. Get her on the phone, pronto."

"One moment, please," Bruce said calmly. He placed the phone down and set off to find Christina. She was coming down the stairs, a load of photo albums in hand. "You have a call. Your ex," he told her.

"Oh, God. Bella," she said, thrusting the books into his arms. Bruce caught everything and followed her. She'd grabbed the phone by the time he'd reached the kitchen. "Kyle?"

She put a finger to her lips and gestured to the table. Bruce placed the photo albums down but didn't take a seat. "That's my law partner. We're working on the case. What? I was upstairs in the bathroom. I do have bodily functions, you know. No, I don't have a phone in there the way you do, nor do I want one."

Stress firmed Christina's shoulders into a straight line and her lips pursed as she listened. Bruce unclenched his fists to free some of his own tension. "No, Kyle. Oh, good grief. You're kidding me. Let me guess. You can't handle it. Oh, why do I even bother? Let me talk to my daughter. Now."

Bruce shot Christina a curious glance, and she covered the mouthpiece with her hand. "Bella's broken out with chicken pox. I'll need to go get her."

"Why can't he…?"

But Christina had already turned her attention back to the phone. "Hi, honey. Oh, sweetheart, I know you itch. Yes, I know you had the shot. But sometimes you get chicken pox anyway. It just won't be as bad. No, it's not because you ate any chicken strips. I know you planned on going to your dad's game, but you won't be at school, either. I'll have to call Megan's mom. I bet more kids in your class have them. Yes, I'll see you soon. Hand the phone back to your daddy."

Christina covered the receiver. "She has to come home."

"Of course she does," Bruce agreed. When a child was sick, being with a mother like Christina was always the best thing. "When is Kyle leaving?"

"He's not." She listened to Kyle for a second and then said, "I'll be on my way in fifteen minutes." With that she ended the call.

Bruce stared at Christina. "You're not driving to Cincinnati."

His voice must have held a question for she said, "Yes, I am."

He shook his head. "The roads are still too dangerous and it'll be dark by the time you get there. Since it didn't stop snowing until early morning, in some spots only one lane of the highway is open. At some point, the road crews have to go home and take a break before they go back out again. I'm not having you drive an hour-and-a-half round trip in the dark."

"I am getting my child."

"Of course you are. I didn't say you weren't. I said you aren't driving. If you're going, you're riding with me."

She stared at him, but Bruce solidified his stance and crossed his arms. This was one argument he was going to win. "I'll wait in the truck while you go inside Kyle's and get Bella, but don't even bother to argue road conditions with a firefighter. You can call me whatever names you'd like, but on this one I'm not backing down."

"Thank you. I actually hate driving in snow and ice."

Her sudden acquiescence startled him. He faltered as his next argument became unneeded. "Then it's good I'm taking you, because I'm used to snow and have even had training in how to drive a fire truck in this stuff. In fact, last night I did."

Poor recovery, he thought, but his explanation had done the job. Christina was already reaching for her coat, so he dug into his jeans pocket and pulled out the key fob. Within a minute, diesel noise rumbled across the driveway. So much for baby pictures and family albums. Maybe later.

"So tell me," he said as they pulled onto the highway, "why won't Kyle drive her back here?"

"Actually, he wouldn't have been driving her home on Sunday, either. His parents would have brought Bella here after the game. But they have a dinner tonight, so tonight they can't."

"That still doesn't answer my question about why he won't bring her home. I assume he has a car?"

"Four of them," Christina said. "But none that he is willing to take out in this weather. Besides, he said it would interfere with his training schedule."

"What, he can't be enough of a parent to change his schedule to take care of his sick daughter? What kind of a man is he? Wait, don't answer that. You told me he played football the day of Bella's birth."

"I know. I reflect back on my marriage and ask myself, 'What was I thinking?' Really, I must have been crazy. I suppose I wanted what everyone else in my family had, which was someone to love, someone to call mine. Kyle waltzed in, swept me off my feet with fairy-tale promises, and I thought I was in love. Then I learned that my prince only wanted to play with me when it suited him, and then I'd better be properly dressed, etc. It wasn't until Bella arrived that I found someone to love me."

"But she's not always going to be around. She's a child, not a male partner."

"True, but I have a lot of years left. Child-rearing is

like putting yourself through law school. You have to go through the daily grind, and you learn and grow because of it. Then one day, poof. You're done and ready for the world. Raising Bella's like that. One day she'll fly, and I'll be on the ground cheering her the whole way. Like this song."

Bruce pressed the control on his steering wheel, increasing the volume of the country station. Kenny Chesney's vocals on his hit "There Goes My Life" flooded the cab.

"All the dreams of this guy in the song go up in smoke when his girlfriend gets pregnant, but he deals with it. Then he realizes that his life, although different from anything he'd ever wanted or imagined, is worth something after all when his daughter leaves to follow her dreams. He has a higher calling."

Bruce placed his hand on Christina's, weaving his fingers through hers. "You're pretty incredible, you realize that? The way you sacrifice amazes me. I wonder if I'd have it in me."

"Of course you would. You're about to embark on a road trip just so that Bella and I are safe. You're a knight, Bruce. A modern-day knight."

"I'm far from it," he replied gruffly. "Far from it."

And with that, they became silent, letting the more-upbeat tempo of the latest Tim McGraw song transition them to less introspective topics like politics and sports. At last, Bruce drove up into an exclusive enclave of larger homes in the outskirts of Cincinnati. "You lived here?"

"Yes," she said. "It seems so strange every time I come back. For a moment I wonder what the heck I was thinking to give it all up. I can almost hear my mother's gasp of despair. After all, I was married to football's Most Valuable Player."

Bruce drove up to a big set of wrought-iron gates. A security camera turned slightly, and he pressed the talk button.

"Yes?"

"Bruce Lancaster and Christina Jones. We're here to pick up Bella."

Christina leaned over, almost into Bruce's lap. "Let me in," she shouted, her face toward the camera. She then slumped back into her leather seat. There wasn't an answer from the speaker, only a click; but a few seconds later the black gates slowly opened inward.

"Everything will be fine," Bruce said reassuringly. "We'll grab her and go."

Christina exhaled a frustrated breath. "Just keep me from killing him. That's all I ask."

"Hey, I'm not a defense lawyer. Our firm doesn't handle those kinds of criminal cases."

"Not even for me? Not even after you see what a condescending jerk he is? We'll see what he says about my clothes."

She was wearing blue jeans and a sweatshirt. Bruce frowned. "I didn't believe I was coming inside."

"Oh, you're coming inside," Christina insisted, tension rolling off her in waves. "He already knows you're here. His security has let him know, so you might as well satisfy his twisted curiosity. Just be sure to trash his ego."

"We're guys. We're not supposed to do that kind of stuff even to the wrong sort. It's in the code."

"When you meet him, you'll break the code, believe me. Oh, his parents are here. I thought they'd have left by now. It's almost five. Great. You can meet the whole Jones clan."

"A flurry of activity" was the best way Bruce could describe the next fifteen minutes. If anyone had been expecting Bella to race down the long, curving marble stairs, shrieking "Mama," they'd have been sorely disappointed.

Instead, a man Bruce recognized from the news as Kyle's agent opened the large etched-glass front door. "Christina," he said simply as he admitted them into the oversize, two-story-high foyer that could have graced the cover of *Architectural Digest*.

"Nate," she replied tightly. Her greeting had been only one word, but Bruce now knew enough about Christina to recognize that she couldn't stand the man.

"There you are." As the agent shut the door behind them, Kyle's mother walked into the room, her long ballgown swishing at her feet. Her hair was piled on the top of her head, and she had a double strand of pearls at her throat. "I'm sorry, Christina. Except for a few residual sniffles this morning, she seemed fine. I feel terrible that we have to attend the charity ball. We can't get out of it, or you know I'd take care of her."

"It's okay," Christina said. "I'll just get her and then you and Duke can be on your way."

"Between you and me, Duke doesn't really want to attend."

But instead of listening, Christina was halfway up the stairs. She paused and turned back. "Bruce?"

At that moment, seeing her alone on the large staircase, he realized that what she'd said was true. He was her knight. He'd scale walls, climb the highest mountains and slay the largest dragons for her, and all without her loving him back in the slightest. Ms. Boxing Gloves was in the ring, and she needed him in her corner. And by God, he was going to be there.

"I don't think so," Nate began, but Christina stopped him smoothly.

"Nate, Bruce works with me at Lancaster and Morris. He's one of the top legal minds in the field. I finally found myself the best. Besides, he kickboxes with underprivileged children and fights fires for fun. He's not a man to mess with in any capacity." Christina smirked slightly and waited for Bruce to catch up. Kyle's mother simply stood there, stupefied.

"Padding my résumé a bit?" he whispered as they climbed the stairs.

"Nate's a snake," Christina replied. "He's probably running off to find Kyle now. Kyle doesn't make a move without him. Nate is the type of guy who understands the idea of bite or be stomped on. Bella is in this part of the house. She kept her old room. Except for toys and clothes, I was the one who bought all new stuff."

"I can't imagine how hard a decision it was for you to leave," he said. "I'm glad you made it."

"It was the worst thing I ever had to do. There's no easy way to say that mommy and daddy don't live together anymore and pretty much can't stand each other. But as this was Kyle's home before I met him, I chose to leave and take Bella. Trust me, I didn't fit into my next neighborhood, either."

"Mama?" a groggy voice called, and Christina rushed into the pink bedroom.

"I'm here, sweetheart. Let's get you home, splotchy girl."

"They itch," Bella complained.

"I know. We'll put you in a nice hot bath with some special ingredients to make you feel all better. Plus you can take your cherry-flavored medicine. That will help, too."

Christina was putting antihistamine and colloidal oatmeal into terms a child could understand. Pride brimmed within him. She was certainly something. Unable to keep silent, Bruce said, "Hey, Bella." The red bumps tugged his heartstrings.

"Bruce!" Her little face brightened. He and Colin had had chicken pox at the same time, so Loretta Morris had pretty much insisted that Bruce stay at her place. Bruce's mother hadn't minded; after his sister's death she'd never been really good with illness, even the common cold.

"I've had chicken pox," Bruce announced, "so you and I can play together. In fact, I'm going to bring my video game system over for your television if it's okay with your mom."

Christina glanced up sharply from where she sat by Bella's side. "Oh, Mama. Please?"

"Okay," she said slowly.

"Great. I've got lots of E-rated games you and I can do together." Well, he didn't, but he knew exactly where to go borrow them. Between the Morris sisters and their respective broods, they had everything.

"You don't have to do this," Christina said as she rose to her feet.

"Yes, I do," Bruce insisted. "And this is not the time or place to discuss it. Let's get her home."

"My coat's downstairs," Bella said, her splotchy face reddening more with a million tears. "I wanted to play in the snow."

"And when you're a little better, you can, even with chicken pox," Christina said. She moved to the closet, took out a suitcase and began putting Bella's personal things inside.

Bruce sat down on the edge of the bed, next to Bella. "It's not supposed to melt for a while," he told her. "And it's dark. Maybe next week when you're not at school, I'll help you make a snowman."

"I'm missing school?"

"Yep. You can't go until all the spots scab over. That's the rules." Bruce touched his forefinger to the end of her nose, which magically remained pox free. Bella attempted to giggle, but wasn't quite up to it. "Now, it's a long drive to your house, and you'll be in the back of my truck, okay? Are you hungry, because I guarantee that once you get inside the truck, the rumbling will make you go to sleep."

"Your truck rumbles?" Bella said, her eyes wide. "Like the fire truck?"

"Yep, but not as loud," Bruce said. "The fire truck's diesel engine is much bigger than mine."

"I think I've got everything that I sent," Christina announced as she scrutinized the room one more time. "Honey, you'll need to get dressed."

"She'll be fine," Bruce said. "Let me carry her out. I left the truck running, so it'll be warm. Bella, did you know that diesel engines aren't happy if you turn them off and turn them right back on in cold weather?"

He had her hooked. "No," she said.

"It's best to let them run. So my truck's already nice and warm. We'll just put some slippers on you here, and your mom can pack your shoes. All that's missing is your winter coat."

"Downstairs," Bella said again. She reached over and clutched a stuffed cat to her side. "Can't forget special kitty."

"Of course not," Bruce said, and he hoisted Bella into his arms. "Gosh, you are a big girl."

"I'm sixty-eight pounds!" Bella proclaimed. "I weighed myself last night on Daddy's scale."

"You must be full of turkey," Bruce said as he carried Bella through the open doorway. He turned around for a moment, his gaze on the luggage. "Do you have that? I can come back for it."

"I've got it," Christina said, carrying Bella's travel luggage. "Let's just get her home."

They reached the foyer without incident, and surprisingly, it was empty. Perhaps Nate had made himself scarce and Kyle's parents had left. Christina set the suitcase down. "I'll be back in a second."

"Mama is getting my coat," Bella explained. "Daddy has a whole room of coats by the kitchen."

Speaking of the man, wasn't he even going to come out and say goodbye to his daughter? If Bruce had had a daughter, he would have. And what was taking Christina so long?

SHE'D ALMOST MADE IT. She'd grabbed Bella's coat and mittens from the coatroom, gotten safely through the kitchen and had been tackled in the hall. What was it about hallways lately?

"We need to talk," Kyle said. Christina could see Nate hovering in a doorway a few doors down. He was trying to be unobtrusive and discreet, and failing miserably.

"I don't have time right now, and especially not when Nate thinks he can eavesdrop."

Nate's head disappeared behind the doorway, but Christina knew he was still there, watching out for his precious client.

"I don't like you introducing Bella to strange men," Kyle said without preamble.

Christina stared at him, her jaw dropping in disbelief. He hadn't changed much since she'd seen him last: same good looks even when he was wearing black jeans and a Bengals sweatshirt. But now she could see the man he truly was, especially when compared with someone as kind and caring as Bruce.

"Oh, good grief! I do not believe you. You, the man who runs a revolving door of bimbos, has the nerve to tell me what to do? My daughter just a while ago told me she missed—oh, what was her name? Elanna—because you'd left her. Bella's not sure whom you're dating at any given time, just that your women become discarded playthings. As if that's any example to set for your daughter. Just consider this. Would you ever want your daughter to date or sleep with someone like you?"

"Beside the point," Kyle said, rallying, ignoring the argument. "The point remains—"

To hell with being polite. "The point remains that I'm someone you can't control, and you hate that," Christina cut in. "As for Bruce, we work together and are friends. If that's a problem, let's go back to court. I get free legal services now. Did you know that one of the firm's partners won a Supreme Court case? Really, Kyle, the phrase 'Know when to say when' applies to more than beer."

Her chest heaved and she took a deep breath. The gloves were on and she was far from finished. "As for being a father, you can't even manage to deal with chicken pox interrupting your precious training schedule. How Peyton Manning manages to balance a successful career and family is simply beyond me, when you obviously can't do it. Perhaps Nate can get you some tips, since I can see your agent is back to hovering in doorways. Now, excuse me. Our daughter is sick, and I'm taking her home."

With that, Christina stormed out into the foyer, her blond hair flying around her shoulders from the combination of static and adrenaline.

"Did he insult your outfit?" Bruce asked.

"No." Christina took another deep breath. Seeing Bruce standing there, holding Bella, the suitcase at his feet, calmed her somewhat. This man, whether she liked the situation or not, had taken over her future. And that wasn't necessarily a bad thing.

She wasn't quite sure how to handle this new grind. Nothing was normal; nothing was going as planned. She was to move to Morrisville, become a great lawyer and raise her daughter. Bruce had complicated things.

Once again she'd put on her boxing gloves and dueled with Kyle. At least she was winning more and more rounds. Perhaps that was something. Like Scarlett O'Hara, though, she chose to think about it tomorrow. "Ready?" she asked Bruce.

Bruce arched an eyebrow at her but only said, "Ready."

"I am," Bella said, and within moments, her coat on, the trio stepped out into the cold but star-filled night and headed home.

CHRISTINA SPOKE LITTLE on the way, even less after Bruce drove the truck into her driveway and they took Bella inside, fed her some soup and tucked her into bed.

She'd fallen asleep almost immediately, though it wasn't yet eight.

Christina didn't want him there, but Bruce also saw that, at the same time, she didn't want him to go. A woman confused—that was his Christina.

"So much for photo albums," Christina said as she came back down the stairs. "I've taken way too much of your day. Thank you."

A dismissal, but he wasn't going to take it. "You're welcome. And don't feel guilty. It's my job to rescue you—everything from a smoke machine to an insensitive husband."

"It's not your job," she said.

Oh, but it was, ever since she'd laid unconscious claim to him. He reached for her hand, taking it in his. Her fingers trembled beneath his and he led her into the family room. "I'm a volunteer, remember. So I've drafted myself. You don't even have to sign me up. I'm already there."

"You're too kind," she said simply. He eased her down onto the sofa and tugged off her boots. "Another foot massage? You're going to spoil me."

"I intend to," he said simply, drawing her legs across his lap and beginning to remove her socks. "Get used to it."

"It's not fair," she said, and Bruce watched as those gorgeous brown eyes closed in blissful satisfaction when he rubbed his thumbs under her instep.

"Life's not fair," he whispered. "Sometimes, though, you do get what you need."

"Perhaps," she agreed, her head lolling to one side. His heart went out to her. She was tired. "Maybe it takes a lot of frogs to find a prince, or bumpy roads or...."

"Maybe," Bruce agreed as she lost the words to convey her jumbled thoughts. "Maybe for some life comes easy, but for the rest of us, it's more rewarding later after all our mistakes led to perfection. Trial and error to finally get it right."

"But how do you know it's right?" Christina asked. "How do you know that this time life hasn't handed you just another wrong turn, another dead end?"

"You just do," Bruce said. "You just do."

"I would have expected you to say you don't," she said.

"I'm nothing like you expected."

Christina opened her eyes and turned her head toward him. Since he'd shifted positions, his gaze locked with hers over a tiny distance of ten inches. "No, you're not. You're much more. It scares me."

"I'm man enough to admit that you scare me right back. You are so beautiful," he said, running a forefinger down her soft cheek. "And it's not because you're pretty on the outside, which you are. You're also beautiful on the inside. It's in your new toughness, the way you'll fight like a lioness over her cub. It's in the way you try to make the world a better place, as you did for those women last night when you treated them like equals and fed them dinner at the country club. It's in the way you smile, the way your mind works, the way this line right here—" he touched it "—creases when you're mad. You are the most competent and diverse female I've ever met, Christina."

He'd overwhelmed her, and a tear freed itself from the corner of her right eye. He gently flicked it away with his forefinger and used the wetness to trace her lower lip.

"We can't be friends, can we?" she asked, already knowing the answer.

"No," he said simply, his smile so very gentle. "We're destined for much more than that as soon as you stop fighting it."

"I'm not ready."

"I know," he said. "You have a few more battles to fight, a few more wars inside yourself to win."

"You can't wait for me. I may never be ready. I didn't even learn to swim until I was ten. Quite odd for living in Houston, where everyone has pools they can swim in year-round if they're kept heated."

He reached forward and silenced her lips with the tip of his finger. Its coarse texture felt so good, so fitting, that her lips parted, although not to speak. He leaned closer, his face hovering over hers, his breath sweet against her cheek.

And then, for the first time, Bruce's mouth found hers.

Lips like sugar. The thought flickered in Christina's consciousness before her mind and heart focused only on Bruce's sensual kiss.

His lips were light, sweet and, oh, so infinitely tantalizing. He nipped her lips with his teeth. His tongue darted against her lower lip, wetting and tasting before sliding slickly inside her mouth to explore its hidden crevices.

And at all times he was nothing but tender. This was not a kiss to plunder, not a kiss to possess, not a kiss to provoke. This was a kiss to pleasure, to plead.

It was a kiss of hello and of goodbye rolled into one. A kiss of remembrance, of letting go and starting anew. It was everything and more.

Christina heard herself whimper. She could lose herself in this man. He could sweep her away, make her pretend that everything was okay. All it would take was one more kiss—

"Mama?"

Christina jolted, her head banging against the couch and crashing into Bruce's chin on the rebound. He grunted in pain, but already she was pushing him aside, her feet hitting the ground and moving quickly toward the stairs. She found Bella at the top. "I had a bad dream, Mama. And I itch." Bella's hand went for her arm.

"Stop. Don't scratch. I have some special spray to make it better." Christina took the steps two at a time. "Come with me."

She led Bella into the bathroom. "I got to go," Bella announced as they reached the bathroom door.

"I'll be just a moment," Christina said. "Go on in, honey."

Christina closed the door behind her daughter and went to the top of the stairs. Bruce stood at the foot, his black leather jacket already on. He was leaving. "Bella's awake," she said unnecessarily.

Bruce gave her a wry smile and put two fingers to his lips, then blew her a kiss as if sending it on the wind. But they still needed to talk. So much had happened today. While the evening had to end, it couldn't end like this.

She started down, but her daughter's voice again stopped her. "Mama?"

"I just wanted to give you your privacy," Christina called. "Hold on. I'm coming, honey."

First, though, she had to tell Bruce she was sorry. But when she turned around, all that greeted her was an infusion of fresh, cold air.

Bruce had already gone.

# Chapter Eleven

He was true to his word. Although Bruce and Christina worked from her home for the duration of Bella's chicken pox, after that kiss Bruce reverted to law partner.

Not that he didn't bring Bella a game system and endless video games the day after that mind-drugging kiss.

But in the weeks that followed, he treated Christina with almost hands-off, professional courtesy. He once again became the workaholic lawyer he was reputed to be.

That was not the way Christina wanted it, although she'd rationalized that maybe it was for the best.

Yet she hated not knowing what was behind those deep-blue eyes when she caught him studying her.

As for the case, that had been their only common ground, except that Bruce said very little about it, too. Even after the meeting with Elaine Gray and the team of lawyers retained by the Morrisville Garment Company ended in disaster, he didn't discuss things with Christina.

He'd expected the negotiations to fail; that she knew.

Morrisville Garment had refused to consider the women's demands, even after Bruce had told them that he had obtained the right-to-sue letter from the EEOC. The company still maintained their innocence, that their supervisors had not created a hostile work environment. With no settlement forthcoming, Bruce had simply stood and walked out, leaving Christina and Angela scrambling to pick up documents and follow him out the door.

He hadn't apologized or explained, but Christina hadn't expected him to, even after the fact. When Bruce was working, he was like Roy Lancaster in one regard—he was a master at putting on a show. His abrupt departure had told Christina how determined Bruce was. The action had had the same effect on the Grays, although they still refused to settle.

One hundred and fifty dollars of Lancaster and Morris's money later, the class-action suit about multiple Title VII violations had been filed in federal court the very next day. The news media instantly picked up on the case, and after a brief conference, Bruce and Christina handled the press conference together.

Reginald Morris declared it a success, that the media bias was solidly in Lancaster and Morris's favor.

Now the legal fury really began, as all women in the suit had to sit for formal depositions in the presence of a court reporter. Bruce planned on subpoenaing many of the garment company's management staff, as well.

Because of the upcoming Christmas holiday, during which Morrisville Garment would be shut down from Christmas Eve through New Year's day, the Lancaster and Morris team had postponed the start of depositions and related discovery until the second week of January.

With the holidays drawing closer, Christina made flight arrangements to head to Houston the day after Christmas. As for Bruce, she had little idea what he'd be doing during her absence. They'd kept their communications on two topics: Bella and the case.

Christina found herself not liking it one bit.

The man had truly set her aside.

Not that his feelings weren't still there. She sensed them when he looked at her—the hunger that couldn't be assuaged. He just hid them well. He was giving her time and space.

And she was discovering she didn't want or need either. Work didn't keep her warm, and the file folders that occupied Christina's bed until late at night didn't satisfy. She'd trapped herself in a web of her own making.

She was on her first big case, and all she felt was frustration at how things were going. Worse, she'd had a sense of solidarity with Angela, and Angela was starting her maternity leave on Christmas Eve. The replacement paralegal came highly recommended, and Angela was training her, but the workload had already reduced the fresh-faced temp to near tears once, when she hadn't been able to find things in the time frame Bruce referred to as "the Angela standard."

Frankly, Christina missed Bruce. She missed the rapport. Simply, he'd become a fixture, one she was fast discovering she didn't like being without.

He meant something to her, and when she let the

door close at her house that fateful night, she'd chosen the safe and narrow. She'd chosen to remain alone.

"MAMA, ARE WE THERE YET?"

"Almost, sweetheart," Christina said. It was the day after Christmas, and they'd boarded the plane that morning in Cincinnati. Bella had been bored a half hour into the flight. "Out the window you can see Galveston Bay and the chemical plant spires."

"They're ugly," Bella said, craning her neck so she could see out the airplane window. "I like Morrisville better."

"You haven't seen Morrisville from the air," Christina pointed out. "And it'll be warmer here. You can even swim in *abuelita's* pool."

"I'll swim in the summer," Bella said. "I like the snow better."

"Hush, don't let *abuelita* hear you say that. She thinks the white stuff is scary. You should have heard her when Houston got snow in 2004. She wouldn't leave the house until it all melted."

Bella giggled at this picture of Christina's mother. "She'd hate where we live."

"Which is why she'll only come to visit us in the summer, when it's warm," Christina said. She ruffled Bella's hair as the 767's wheels hit the ground with a jolt. For the first time in years, as the plane screeched to a stop and taxied to the gate, Christina didn't experience a sense of homecoming. How odd to think that in three short months Morrisville had become her home and that her childhood town of Houston now belonged firmly in her past. Once she'd missed it with a passion. Now it was simply a place to visit.

"*¡Hola!* Christina. *¡Hola!* Bella." Christina's brother, Enrique, waited just outside security. He looked well, she noticed. It took forty minutes to gather their luggage, and soon the bags were in the back of Enrique's SUV and they were on their way to the family home in an affluent Hispanic section of Houston.

"So Santa stopped here, too?" Bella asked. Santa had been very generous this Christmas.

"He did, and he even left you some presents," Enrique confirmed, as they drove onto Christina's parents' street. Poinsettias lined walkway after walkway and porch after porch. "You'll find them under the tree."

"He also came to my house," Bella told her uncle. "That's why we couldn't fly in until today. Mama said we should spend Christmas in our house this year so Santa would know where we moved to. He slid down the chimney and ate all the milk and cookies I left."

"You like Morrisville?" Enrique asked, his question directed at his sister.

"I do," Christina replied honestly. "I'm comfortable there, much more so than I was in Cincinnati, and Bella's in a great elementary school."

"I have lots of friends," Bella declared. "And I earned a lot of Brownie try-its already."

"Badges," Christina explained.

"That's great," Enrique said. "As long as you're both happy."

"We are," Christina replied, and as the words left her lips, she knew they were true. She wasn't giddily happy, but she was content. And contentment could be permanent, whereas euphoria ended. Except for the situation with Bruce—and the jury was still out on how to handle that—Christina realized that her life was how she'd wanted it all along. She had finally reached normal.

Yet something was missing.

A few minutes later they were enveloped in hugs as Christina's family poured out the front door to greet her and Bella.

It wasn't until New Year's Eve, though, that the inquisition in the shape of her mother caught up with Christina. The house was packed with friends and relatives. The immediate family had celebrated privately with the main meal of the day around two, and a light buffet had been set in the dining room for all the guests who flowed throughout the house. Christina reached for a plastic cup. The multitude of beverage selections included orange juice, and at this moment that sounded perfect.

"Christina Miranda, I've been trying to get you to myself all week." Christina's mother materialized at her elbow, and Christina managed not to spill her drink. Christina had always stood seven inches taller than her five-foot-two parent, and whenever her mother called out Christina's full name, Christina would ready herself. Her mother's lips puckered into a pout of disappointment. "We haven't had one good conversation since you arrived."

"*Mami,* I'm sorry," Christina said. She couldn't add

the lie that it wasn't intentional. Talking to her mother was always like talking to a tsunami. It washed over you and left years' worth of damage.

"I was disappointed that you arrived after the holiday. You missed the *posada*. Bella would have loved being part of the procession. We try to maintain traditions around here."

"I couldn't get a decent flight out of Cincinnati until afterward," Christina said. "Anyway, you always say that all the good pilots don't work the holidays and so not to fly on those days. Spending Christmas in Morrisville gave me some time alone with Bella."

"You should have been here, flying earlier if necessary," her mother said, refusing to concede the point. "You're letting Bella forsake her heritage. She only sees us twice a year."

"She speaks Spanish, *Mami,* and she knows who everyone in the family is. I have pictures, and I am not going to take Bella to Mexico to see distant relatives until she's older and can remember the trip. Not to mention that Kyle is her father and he has rights, as well. She is part of two cultures, and we live in a town that, for the most part, is culturally blind."

"America is never culturally blind. We created our own enclave here, yes, and we have grasped the American dream and molded our own. But we do not forget where we come from."

"*Mami,* that's all well and good. But Bella comes from the here and now, as well. She is a child. And our family hasn't struggled in the past century. Even in

Mexico. If you want to see struggle and the attempt to make a better life, I have several women you should meet. Just leave your designer clothes at home. They'll never be able to afford them, and to wear them adds insult to injury—they probably made them. Besides, Kyle and I have joint custody of Bella. We have to share the holidays. And this year I thought it was important Bella and I spend Christmas in our home and start our own tradition."

She'd mentioned her ex again, and her mother pounced. "I never should have let you go off to Harvard. It all started there."

"I had a scholarship to one of the best law schools in the country. I was going no matter what. I wanted to be an attorney and I am. Kyle was just a detour on the way to what I want for myself. And the result is my beautiful child, without whom I cannot imagine my life. So there is a silver lining in every situation."

*Mami* seemed to concede this point, for she changed the subject. "What about current prospects? Someone to share this post-Kyle life with. Have you spoken to Manuel? He's here tonight. You should go chat. You know he was always interested in you."

"No." Christina's tone was harsh. "*Mami,* I am not about to begin a long-distance relationship just because Manuel comes from an appropriate family."

Her mother squared her shoulders. "He's ready to settle down. He just got promoted to vice president of his firm. It's not right for you to be single."

"And why is it not right for me to be single? Does it

carry a stigma? Because my marriage failed, then I failed? If so, half the people in this country are failures. And I can't buy or believe that."

"I just want you happy," her mother insisted.

"Then let me be happy. I'm old enough to find happiness by myself. As for Manuel, I am not interested," Christina said firmly, meaning every word.

Sure, Manuel could turn heads a mile away, but all this week her thoughts had drifted to what a single, dark-haired volunteer firefighter might be doing. He'd haunted her.

Her mother made one last attempt. "Christina…."

"I have my life, *Mami,* and while I love you dearly and respect your intentions, you must respect that I'm a big girl and can forge my own path."

"You've messed up," Christina's mother said, her brown eyes brimming.

Ah, tears to yank the heartstrings. But this time they weren't going to work. Still, Christina pulled her mother into a tight embrace. "And that's part of life. You raised me, but now it's my turn to live on my terms."

"It seems so odd," her mother said.

"Millions of women do it daily. Work keeps me very busy, and that's what I choose to do—carve my own path, not share someone else's."

"I just don't want you to be alone."

"I'm not. I have Bella and…"

*And I have Bruce,* Christina had been about to say. But she didn't have him. They could only be friends in the context of being lovers. And she'd turned him away.

The realization that she was *not* okay with what she'd done sent Christina reeling. She'd been so blind.

"Are you all right?" Her mother peered up at her.

"Of course," Christina lied. "I'm just a little tired. Bella's been sick, and looking after her was exhausting."

"Drink more orange juice," her mother said, refilling Christina's cup.

"Thank you." Christina moved a step away. "I'm going to check on Bella."

But Christina didn't try to locate Bella. Instead, she found a quiet corner. She wanted Bruce Lancaster. Well, she'd known that for a while. But tonight she'd realized she couldn't *stand* not having him. He had to be in her life.

There were worse things than living alone, and one was living in fear. That was exactly what she'd been doing. She'd been letting her uncertainties paralyze her. To live, she had to risk.

If this had been a soap opera, or even a romantic movie, Christina would have been making her excuses, running through the airport, catching the next plane and rushing to be in Bruce's arms. They'd spend the rest of the night making love and satiating themselves.

But neither scenario was reality, as the little hand tugging on hers demonstrated. "Mama, I've been searching for you. Cousin Christopher says that we're shooting off fireworks tonight."

"We are," Christina said.

"Goodie," Bella said. She tugged on her mother's hand again. "Do you think that they're doing fireworks in Morrisville?"

"I don't know," Christina said. "Maybe next year we'll be there and we can find out."

"Bruce told me he was going to a big party at the country club. He said that was where everyone goes, but it's not for kids."

*Mami* walked up at this moment and overheard the last portion of the conversation. "Who's Bruce?"

"One of the junior partners in my firm," Christina answered. "We're the two principal attorneys on the Title VII case."

"Oh," her mother said, obviously disappointed. She'd been wondering if Bruce was a potential prospect.

"He's hunky," Bella said. "He put out the fake fire at my school."

"He's also a firefighter?"

"Volunteer," Christina said. "The job is an honor in Morrisville. Family tradition. And there wasn't a fire. A smoke machine set off the alarm. Bella was never in any danger."

"He showed us the fire truck," Bella continued, her eyes glowing with admiration for Bruce. "And when I was sick, he brought me video games to play."

"He sounds more than just a law partner."

"That's just the kind of man he is," Christina said. "Besides, I had to work from home, so if he hadn't come by, we would have fallen behind on the case."

"You should marry him, Mama," Bella announced suddenly.

"It's a little more complicated than that," Christina told her daughter.

"How so?" Bella asked.

"You'll understand when you're grown-up."

Christina's mother simply arched a black eyebrow, her question unspoken. Christina checked her wristwatch. The digital time display provided an immediate diversion. "It's 10:50. Shouldn't we start rounding everyone up for the fireworks? It's still tradition in this neighborhood to start an hour before midnight and end at twelve, isn't it?"

"Yes," her mother answered. "Amazing how traditions work."

And so convenient, Christina thought.

"Fireworks," Bella shrieked, and danced off to find her cousins.

"We will talk about all this later," her mother said before she stepped away.

Christina's smile tightened. Not if she could help it.

THEY WERE SHOOTING the fireworks off at midnight. The Morrisville Country Club always put on a huge display, and the temperature had freakishly warmed up to forty degrees. The melting snow meant the grounds were soggy, so most people who ventured outside would crowd the patio and watch as the fireworks exploded over the sixth green.

Bruce brushed some lint off his tuxedo lapel. Why he'd let Colin talk him into attending this boring bash was beyond him. Bruce couldn't care less. Oh, the food had been good, and he'd danced a little and socialized, but being here reminded him of Christina and the Thanksgiving party she'd hosted.

He could still picture her smile, the way her wheat-colored hair wisped around her shoulders. He still had her carnation on his dresser.

"I brought you more champagne for the toast. It's traditional to share champagne and a kiss."

"Oh. Thanks," Bruce said absently, accepting the glass from the woman, who was his date for tonight only. She was Colin's escort's younger sister, and the blind date was fast going to hell.

"You're welcome," she said, fluttering her lashes. Inwardly Bruce groaned. He'd kill Colin for this later. Colin and Kate were on the dance floor, slow dancing without a space between them. Kate Kendall was a former Miss Indiana; her sister was equally beautiful.

Bruce wasn't interested in the slightest.

"Bruce, would you like to dance?"

Bruce set the glass she'd brought him on a nearby table. He had no desire for champagne, especially since he knew he hadn't misread any of her signals all night. Now, after the latest, he was certain. Time to finish this farce.

"Linda, you're a sweetheart for asking me to dance, but I've been ruined by someone else and that's not fair to you."

"What?" The twenty-three-year-old girl's green eyes widened in surprise. It was obviously not the answer she'd been expecting.

"Ruined. I shouldn't have even attempted to come out tonight."

"Kate and Colin told me you've been sulking. I don't

mind." Linda slithered forward and tugged on one of the tuxedo jacket's buttons. "I'm sure I can fix it."

Oh, he might have been interested BC—Before Christina. The man he was BC would have taken Linda up on everything she offered.

The man he was After Christina could love only one woman, and she was in Houston.

"Linda, I'm sorry, but I can't. I respect you, and myself. This is really awkward and sounds cliché, but I'm in love with someone. And while I could indulge myself with you and I'm sure we could share a pretty phenomenal night, I'm not that kind of guy. After the fireworks, I'll drive you home."

"She's a lucky woman," Linda said, her voice controlled and tight. Bruce could tell she wasn't the type used to being rejected, but that wasn't his concern.

"So what's going on?" Colin asked as he and Kate left the dance floor.

"He's in love with someone else," Linda announced with an erratic wave of her hand. "This double date is an absolute bust."

"I never said he'd fall for you," Kate said, seeing her evening with Colin starting to head south. "This was just so you didn't have to stay home alone on New Year's Eve. Colin and I—"

"Yeah, it's all about Colin," Linda shot back.

Bruce winced. This was turning ugly, even more so now that Colin had him in target range.

"You're in love with someone? Are you making that up? Who is it?" Colin said, ignoring the squabbling women. "You're not dating anyone, to my knowledge."

"I don't tell you everything," Bruce said tightly.

"The fireworks are starting," someone next to them shouted.

"You don't have to ruin my night just because he's not interested," Kate was saying. "You can't have every guy you see. This is pointless. I didn't buy this gown for nothing. Colin, fireworks." Kate grabbed his hand.

"I'm not finished talking to you," Linda shouted.

"Later," Kate snapped, and they left Bruce and Linda standing there.

"Come on," Bruce said. "I'll take you home."

"I'll stay," she said with a huff. "I'm not going anywhere with you. There has to be some way to salvage this worthless evening. Kate and Colin can drop me off."

"Your call," Bruce said. As Linda headed for the terrace, he strode for the exit doors.

A vibration began suddenly in his jacket pocket, but for once Bruce wasn't in the mood for the fire department. Some drunk had probably splattered himself and his car all over the road. Some New Year's Eve this was turning out to be.

He'd spent the past few weeks trying to give Christina space when he wanted to simply draw her into his arms and kiss her. But he didn't want to win her through sexual means. So he'd withdrawn. Treated her clinically and professionally. And that had not reduced his feelings at all. It had simply made the situation even crazier.

He pulled the still-vibrating phone from his pocket,

at the same time handing the coat-check attendant his claim ticket. He frowned as he read the cell phone display. A 281 number he didn't recognize.

Who besides the fire department would phone him this late? He snapped open his cell and identified himself. "Lancaster."

"Bruce?" The voice seemed hesitant, almost as if the person was surprised he'd picked up. In a rare moment of shock and clumsiness, he dropped the phone.

The caller was Christina.

# Chapter Twelve

"Hey," she said when he returned to the line.

"Hi," he replied, his voice clear. "How are you?"

Christina clutched the receiver, her knuckles whitening. Everyone else was outside on the street. The whole neighborhood had turned out and everyone would take turns shooting off fireworks from the cul-de-sac until midnight. She'd begged off, citing a headache.

"I'm good," she said. "Did I get it right? Is it midnight there? They were about to drop the Times Square ball on TV before I called."

"It's midnight here," Bruce said. He could hear the fireworks starting to boom, and a distant chorus of "Auld Lang Syne."

"I wanted to hear your voice at midnight," she whispered, and something inside Bruce stirred.

"Happy New Year, Christina," he said.

"Is it?" she said. "Is it going to be happy?"

"Depends on your resolutions." Oh, how he wanted to just lay how he felt flat-out! But she'd phoned him.

This was a path she had to walk herself. He couldn't go to her. She had to come to him.

"I haven't made any resolutions, except…."

"Except what?" he prodded. Now was not a time to let her pause.

"You're supposed to be with the ones you care about on New Year's. At midnight. And with Bella here and you there, I sort of figured…."

For a lawyer who was trained to speak, her argument, her persuasive speech, was bombing—big-time. *Please,* she thought, *say something. Please make this a little easier for me.*

Bruce must have picked up her telepathy. "I'm glad you called," he said. "You see, I was just leaving the country club. I would rather have been alone than with someone I didn't care about."

Jealousy flared. Had he been with someone else? She had no right to know. She'd turned him away. And if there was any hope left… "I care about you," Christina admitted, the words coming out in a rush.

"As a friend," he said.

"No," she whispered. That much had become clear tonight. "No." She was more forceful this time as she gained momentum. "You were right. We can never be friends. Not without everything else. I realized that tonight."

He waited, giving her a few moments to gather her thoughts and put them into words.

Christina loosened her grip on the phone. Most men would have said, *So what do you mean?* or *What's next?* But not Bruce. He was so different from other men. Perhaps that was what made him so perfect—and so difficult. She couldn't follow the old familiar patterns of behavior with him. He'd never played games with her, so the rules of the man-woman-relationship game didn't apply. Nothing in *Cosmo* would save her here. She could only save herself.

"I think I'm ready," she said quietly. "If you still want me."

"Ready?"

"Yes."

"You want me," he said; the lawyer demanding clarification. Christina could respect that.

"Yes." The word came out weakly, but she drew breath. "Yes. I want to try. Take this to the next level. Whatever that entails."

"You're certain." *The chance to back out.*

She waited and let the opportunity pass. "I'm very certain. I'm less sure of how you feel, and if you still want me. Do you know how impossible a relationship between us is going to be?"

"I believe it will be very simple," he said, his reassurance crossing the distance. "Lots of kissing. Lots of hugging. Lots of you, me and Bella hanging out. That's normal, Christina."

Hope flared like a lit firecracker. "Are you saying—"

This time, he interrupted her and she was glad for it. "Christina, I had Miss Indiana's younger sister as my mercy date tonight. She was young, beautiful and absolutely no one I wanted to spend any time with. In fact, she and I parted ways only a few moments before you called. I told her I was in love with someone else."

"In love with someone else?"

Years of being with Kyle had her momentarily thinking there was another party, but she realized her mistake the very same moment he said, "Yes. You. I'm so desperate that I'll take whatever crumb you give me. That's pathetic, really."

"You're not pathetic."

"I am, Christina. I've tried to be as professional as I could be. But I'm in love with you, and I doubt I could ever tire of you. As you say, it will be more complicated than simply lots of hugging and lots of you, me and Bella hanging out. I'm expecting you don't want anyone to know, and I want to shout it from the rooftops."

"Please, not that. My relationship with Kyle was so public. Bruce, we work together. If we fall apart in two weeks, it will be awkward for everyone at the firm. I've just moved here. I can't uproot Bella again. If I were single, I wouldn't fear as much. But Kyle was such a whirlwind. My marriage went south. My whole life changed on a dime. I can't go through that again. If we're to do this, you must give me time."

"I've been giving you time," he said. "Space."

"I need a different kind. Time together, but just as us. Please. This is hard for me. I want you. I…" She paused. "I need you. I think of you all the time. But I'm scared. It must go slow. It's a paradox, I suppose. I'm such a strong person, but where you're concerned, I've discovered I'm one big chicken. Those fifty-fifty odds seem so overwhelming. And this time I have so much more to lose."

"I know," Bruce said quietly. "Believe me, I know."

"But I want to risk," Christina said, more firmly now. "I want to take a risk and be with you."

"Then we'll concentrate on that," Bruce said, "because I want the same thing."

A silence descended as each considered what to do, what to say now.

"I'm coming home Sunday morning," Christina finally told him. "Can I see you?"

"Of course you can see me. How about we do pizza at your place around five? You, me and Bella. After she goes to bed, we can talk and decide where to go now."

Warmth made her tingly. "I'd like that."

"Then, Christina Jones, go spend the rest of your night with your daughter. I'm going to go home and I will see you on Sunday. It's a date."

A date. She hung up the phone. She had taken the first steps. Small, but forward-moving steps. She remained in control of her future, of her destiny. Maybe she *could* have everything. Maybe it could all be just fine.

"BYE, MOM," Bella said.

"Bye, sweetheart," Christina leaned down and gave Bella a big kiss. "You be a good girl."

"Are you sure you don't mind her spending the night?" Marci asked as Bella ran out of the house and hopped into Marci's minivan. "You just got back from your trip."

"I don't mind," Christina said. "School doesn't start until Wednesday and she hasn't seen Megan in a while. So let them play. I can use the time to work on the case. I'll be working from home until school resumes."

"Okay. You have a good night. I'll bring her back home about noon tomorrow."

"That'll be fine. My law partner may be here, so don't be surprised if you see a big black truck."

"Okay, I won't," Marci said, and with a wave, she and the girls were off. Christina watched the minivan drive out of sight.

Bruce would be the one surprised when he arrived in a few hours. But Marci's phone call and offer to take Bella overnight had been too impossible to resist. Tonight Christina was going to claim the man she had fallen hard for. Tonight she was tossing caution to the wind.

When she opened the door that evening, Bruce's jaw dropped. Christina was wearing nothing but a long, black silky nightgown.

"Come inside. It's cold out there," she said, ushering him into her foyer. "Would you like anything to drink?"

He answered her simply by crushing his lips to hers, his kiss sending her to heaven in an instant. "Do you know how long I've waited for this?" he asked when he surfaced for air.

"How long?" she breathed, her exhalation mixing with his.

"Too long." He lowered his lips to hers for another mind-spiraling kiss. His mouth erased past history and created a new one. She quivered as the sensations he called forth just from a kiss shook her body. His lips nipped and tucked, teased and pulled, sending any regrets and any doubts reeling into infinity. Kissing Bruce Lancaster was better than chocolate, and it wouldn't go to her hips. Only his hands would, and they drew her closer to him.

"This gown has to go. It's driving me mad," he said. "Bella…" he began.

"Won't be home until tomorrow," she said.

"We were going to talk."

"Later," she said.

His answer was a growl as he lowered his mouth to her neck and planted sensual kisses along the side of her throat. He wove his fingers into the silk fabric, hiking it so that her bare legs became visible. Then he simply lifted her into his arms, cradled her against his chest and carried her up the stairs.

"To the left," she whispered, the magnetic power of this man rolling off him in waves. The way he wanted her was evident in the tension of his shoulders, the set of his jaw and the determination in his step.

Never was Bruce anything but tender: his fingers as they plundered; his hands as they pleasured; his arms as they possessed. He slid the strap of the gown over her shoulder blade, his lips following the imaginary line he exposed as the material fell away. They were in the bedroom, and he put her down and bent his head to bring the tip of her breast against the warmth of his tongue. Christina detonated, her body writhing with delight as he suckled her to glorious release before bestowing the same favor on the other straining peak.

He peeled the silky black gown down, exposing her midriff, then spanned her waist with his fingers. And Christina froze with anticipation as he knelt before her and covered this area with kisses, as well. The lingerie pooled around her feet and he worshiped her like a goddess, depositing kisses to her stomach, her thighs and finally the V between her legs.

It was then that he laid her back against the bed, his mouth simply finding a new position as he continued to pleasure her. And then her body bucked and she rode him hard in a release that left her limp. He stood then, at the end of the bed, and she gazed up at him, watching as he began to slowly remove his shirt. She'd never seen anything so deliberate or so sure, his gaze never disconnecting with hers as the shirt fell to the floor, revealing a honed chest, that six-pack stomach and those hard male nipples she craved to touch. His belt went next, a click and a slide as it came undone, a rasp as the zipper slid down. Then the jeans dropped to his feet, and he kicked off shoes and pants to stand clad only in boxers that did nothing to hide his erect state.

And then he was naked, and she couldn't help but reach toward him, her desire to touch him rewarded when he brought himself to her.

He placed himself in her hand, his trust in her ministrations and his groan of enjoyment evident as she stroked.

Making love was all about risk, and as she moved to bring her lips to that most intimate part of him, she knew she was willing to trust Bruce Lancaster not to deliberately hurt her. As her lips slid over him, in a gift she'd refused to bestow on Kyle past his first infidelity, she transferred to Bruce the key to her heart. She gave of herself, not because it was expected but because she wanted to.

She wanted to please this man, to drive him crazy, to make him experience nothing but the passion she could give.

He groaned and slid away, intent on keeping some semblance of control. He turned his attentions fully on her, sending her again into frenzy. He lay beside her, and his mouth and hands roamed her body to rouse her once again. His fingers rubbed, concentrating on her until she was wet, slick and ready.

"I'm on the Pill," she said. She'd been on it for PMS ever since Bella's birth. "I'm safe if—"

He cut her off with a mind-spiraling kiss. "Yearly fire department physical. Clean and yours."

"Then take me," she said, and upon hearing those words, Bruce did.

He slid his length inside her, filling her to the hilt. She closed her eyes, savoring the moment that already threatened to explode into a powerful orgasm. Not that she minded in the least as he brought her to the first crest, held her as she peaked and loved her as she slid down into satisfaction's valley again.

Bruce wasn't in this for his fulfillment, and he held taking anything for his own enjoyment until finally, after many multiple rounds, she urged him on and he obliged her with a pumping release that sent her to the place where she became complete. He throbbed inside her, and she gathered him into her arms, and together they drew breath and lay spent.

"Are you okay?" he whispered, leaving her only to lie next to her side.

Christina marveled at his concern and tenderness. "I'm wonderful. That was wonderful. I…" *It made me special. Yours.*

He read her mind. "It was that way for me, too."

"Thank you," she said. Somewhere she had arms and legs, but as exhausted as her body was after love-making, she could only sense Bruce's fingertips as they traced her eyebrows, nose and lips. She was molten.

"You are so beautiful," he said, and she knew that the words were substitutes for the three little words he wanted to say, words he would leave until she was ready. His thoughtfulness touched her, and she kissed his finger before he withdrew it. She had no idea where the relationship would go, but for now, as he drew a blanket over them, Christina was content. She was in control and the rest would take care of itself.

"So, SLEEPYHEAD, are we getting that pizza at some point?"

Christina sat up so quickly she almost clocked Bruce's chin. He grinned as she missed. "I've learned to move," he said.

"What time is it?" she asked. She had no idea.

"Just turned seven. You haven't been asleep long."

"Oh." It took her a moment to become acclimated to the darkness, and to remember that there was no reason to fear Bella coming in the open door. "You seemed to need some sleep."

"It's been a long while," she admitted. "I...."

"Past," he said. "We only concentrate on the present and future. It's been a while for me, too."

Satisfaction overflowed her at that answer. He wasn't the Casanova of the legal world, no Don Juan out seeking the next thrill.

Without even thinking about it, she began to pet him, stroking his skin in her desire to touch and stay connected.

"That's not the way to get us dinner," he teased, and her brown eyes widened as she saw exactly what effect she was having on him.

About the same as he was having on her. She wanted him. Again. Now. As she took over and began to kiss him, he groaned. Dinner could wait.

"So who is she?"

Bruce lifted his head. Colin stood in the doorway to the small conference room. It was Wednesday, the first day back to school for Bella, and thus the first day that Bruce and Christina had returned to the office to work. Bruce had arrived early; he didn't expect Christina for another half hour.

"Good morning to you," Bruce said.

"Yeah, I guess," Colin said. His expression soured. "For a guy who used to room with me, you've been pretty invisible lately."

"I've been working," Bruce said. "The Title VII case is in full throttle now that we have the right to sue and the case has been filed."

"Excuses," Colin shot back. "It's January fifth and I haven't heard word one from you since you dropped your bombshell."

"Like I said…"

"Work." Colin gave a resigned nod. "You're killing me here, Bruce. Not only did I end up empty on New Year's because Linda and Kate got into a fight, but you also haven't said one word about why you didn't tell me you were in love with someone. Hell, did you think we had to bring her sister? It's amazing how two women can have a row and then find common ground by uniting against some poor guy."

Bruce thought fast. Talking with another lawyer was a lot like playing chess. Each statement had to be thought out; each answer predicted. And this wasn't *any* lawyer. This was Colin. While he wasn't the world's sharpest attorney, he was Bruce's best friend. He had the right to be irritated. They'd been sharing secrets and swapping stories for years. Colin wasn't used to being out of the loop.

"I'm sorry," Bruce said, choosing the easiest path— that of deflection and diversion. "I tried to take her home. It wasn't my intention to ruin your night. You were on a date with Miss Indiana."

"Which fizzled faster than a Fourth of July sparkler. And you didn't answer my question. Who is she?"

Bruce tried another tack. "The sister was making too many moves, and I wasn't interested. So I backed away."

"A state of affairs you've wiggled out of gracefully before. You don't use the L-word, even to extract yourself from sticky situations. So if you said it, you meant it. Maybe the explanation slipped out, but it was truth."

"Close the door," Bruce said.

Colin stepped farther into the small conference room and shut the door behind him. He remained standing, his arms crossed over his chest.

"I am very much in love with someone," Bruce admitted. The Sunday night and Monday morning he'd spent with Christina had been magical. They'd bonded because of chemistry, and bonded further as play turned to work on Monday afternoon after Bella returned. It was now Wednesday, and for the first time in his life, Bruce understood true trepidation. Sure, he fought fires. He jumped into the fray, handled risks every day.

But his relationship with Christina was only four days old, and if anything went wrong, it would vanish quicker than a puff of smoke.

He chose his words to Colin carefully. "This relationship has to be the slowest developing one I've ever endured. She's taking some time to win over. I'm finally making progress, and I'm not about to jeopardize that."

"Okay," Colin drawled in a deliberate attempt to prod for more information. "You didn't do anything at the country club New Year's. But that doesn't tell me who she is."

"It's very complicated. We're being very private, not even telling our parents or best friends. It's not that I don't want to tell you, but I can't. I'm sorry, but that's the way it has to be."

"What, is she ashamed of you? Married?" Colin paused, running through all the scenarios he could think of.

"Stop fishing. I'm not going to take the bait," Bruce stated flatly. "She's special. This is it."

That stopped Colin and he stepped forward sharply. "It? You mean…."

"I'm marrying her," Bruce stated. "As soon as she'll have me."

Colin's eyes narrowed and he scrutinized Bruce. "I don't believe it. You're serious about this."

"Yes," Bruce said simply.

"And you're chasing her."

"Yes. You should try it. Might do you a world of good not to have women fall at your feet."

Colin shrugged off that idea as if he were a horse shaking off flies. "No way. I think you've gone mad. You're chasing her. You may never even catch her. What then?"

"I worry about that. Not all relationships happen in twenty-four hours. Oh, we fought at first, and suddenly the reason was like a punch in the gut. Do you know what it's like having fate just smack you in the face? A giant wake-up call. In one moment I realized that she was it. Everything I'd been wanting and searching for. Yeah, it wasn't in the packaging I'd been expecting. I might have missed it had fate not intervened."

"She's ugly?"

Bruce rolled his eyes. Trust Colin to miss the analogy. Colin was still too much of a playboy to think beyond the box. "No. She's beautiful. But our relationship isn't simply boy meets girl. It's more complicated. All I can say is that I know she's it for me. That means I'll take what I can get. Sometimes you have to hold on for the ride. The good ones may test you first. See if you're noble enough." He remembered Christina's earlier words. "Like a long-term investment."

"This sounds ridiculous," Colin sputtered. "I've never heard you talk like this. Relationships should not be work."

"They're always work. What they shouldn't be is painful."

"You sound like some shrink. We need to continue this later. I've got to get some billable hours in sometime today. How about drinks at the club?"

"Can't," Bruce said. "Plans."

"With her," Colin said.

"Dinner," Bruce confirmed with one word. As Colin shook his head and left the conference room, Bruce glanced at his watch for about the hundredth time in the past ten minutes. Christina should be here any moment. His heart rose a little, thumped faster. How they would make this relationship truly viable was beyond him, but they were going to try.

He'd fallen head over heels in love with his partner. It didn't matter she was his senior partner. Roy had called the other night and announced he'd heard from Adam that Bruce's name was being floated about for a federal judgeship. Eventually, Roy insisted, Bruce would be a judge, the first in Lancaster history. Bruce had let himself dream for a moment, and decided to worry about that if it happened. Reality was the here and now, with Christina and the world he wanted to create with her. Later, once she was secure in their relationship, they'd shout their love from the rooftops. But for now, only four days into it, his loving her and her letting him was more than enough.

COLIN MORRIS LEFT the small conference room with a problem to solve. He was extremely worried about Bruce. He'd never seen him act this way before.

As a kid, Colin had always loved watching detective shows and solving the crime long before the main character did. In college, he'd streamlined the efficiency of the fraternity house in multiple areas, including cleaning. Everyone had been thrilled with that. Colin probably would have made an excellent engineer or scientist—designing things that were solutions to the world's problems. Instead, the Morris boys were lawyers, and Colin found solutions to the chaos people got themselves into.

Bruce had obviously gotten himself into a mess. Colin's best friend thought himself deeply in love. And maybe he was. And because Bruce was twenty-nine, he was a man whose life didn't demand any unwarranted meddling.

But the woman was the unknown variable. Call Colin jaded from the women he dated; call him a skeptic, especially after the recently resolved lawsuit on behalf of an elderly man's family. When their aging father had first started dating the younger woman, the man's children had simply assumed their father, a strong man, could handle it. But when the woman had begun siphoning off more and more money for things like property in her name, designer clothes, joint credit cards, the family stepped in. Except, they stepped in too late. By the time the lawsuit was settled in their favor, their father had lost one million dollars. The money could never be recovered, but at least the woman was gone. Colin had seen too much to accept that Bruce's "love" was rational.

As Colin entered the elevator to his office on the third floor, he began contemplating various scenarios. By the time he emerged from the elevator, he knew where he could find out what he wanted to know.

THE KNOCKING ON THE DOOR caused a picture frame to bounce and made Christina jump. She set her work aside, her interest now on the impeccably dressed man standing in the doorway to her office.

She didn't recognize him. But that didn't stop him. He smiled easily, strode across the room and extended his hand. "Hi, I just realized that we've never met. I'm Colin Morris. My office is down the hall. I'm Reginald's son."

"Hello." Christina did the dutiful thing and rose to her feet. He shook her hand, his grip causing Christina to wince.

"It's great to finally meet you. We've been missing each other these past two months."

"We have," Christina said, her internal radar zinging to full alert. As much as this appeared to be a social call, she knew instinctively it wasn't.

"Have you seen Bruce this morning?" Colin asked as she sat back down.

"No." The door to the small conference room had been closed when she'd gone by, and she assumed he had someone in there with him. She knew he was in the office because his truck was outside in the parking lot.

"Bruce and I go way back," Colin opened easily. "He's more my brother than my best friend. He practically spent every waking moment at my house. We roomed together as undergrads and then as law students."

This she already knew, and she recognized the fishing expedition. The question was what was Colin's motivation? From everything Bruce had told her about Colin, he wasn't the villainous type. Nosy, yes, but not in a nasty way.

"Christina, you've spent more time with Bruce than I have lately, and while this is awkward for me, I don't know where else to turn."

Colin walked to her office door and closed it. "Let me explain. Bruce had a date New Year's Eve. Just a mercy date, the sister of the woman I was seeing."

Christina noted Colin's deliberate emphasis on the word *was*.

"She made some moves, I guess, but nothing Bruce couldn't handle. What he did next, though, was out of character, and frankly, I'm worried. He told Linda— that was her name—that he was in love with someone and that it wasn't honorable for him to lead Linda on. While that's the Bruce I grew up with, it's not like him to use the L-word."

"Maybe he's changed," she said, mentally lacing up the boxing gloves. Just where was Colin going with this, and just what had Bruce revealed? Colin leaned over her desk.

Insecurities raised their ugly heads and she tried to tamp them down. Bruce had wanted her to go public, and she'd refused. Would he honor her wish? Or would he, like most people, let a little "secret" slide to his best friend? Because she hadn't talked to Bruce yet this morning, she had to dance very carefully here. "Maybe he is really in love," she said slowly. "Maybe he has found the woman of his dreams."

"Oh, he is really in love," Colin said. "With you."

"What?" Christina bolted to her feet without thinking about the effect of her movement. "Bruce is a trustworthy man. He never would have said such a thing, even to you."

Colin straightened, his face lacking satisfaction. "No, but you just did."

Her actions had revealed more than words. It was too late to back up, but she tried anyway. "I have no idea what you're talking about."

"Trust me, you've taken his heart. As his best friend, I'm concerned. He's besotted. But your relationship isn't real. It's clandestine—he can't reveal it to anyone. We don't get to share his joy. Why is that?" Colin gestured for emphasis.

She stood stoically still.

"We're both lawyers here. Yeah, I trapped you. But think. If it's this easy for me to figure out your relationship, it's only a matter of time before everyone else does, as well."

"I think you should leave my office," Christina said. She clutched the edge of her desk for support.

Colin shrugged. "Just don't break his heart." With that he turned and left.

Christina slumped into her chair. She'd blown that one, hadn't she? So much for competence or for keeping secrets. Colin had said that Bruce hadn't revealed anything. But she had. One well-placed hit, and she'd fallen like a row of dominoes.

A knock on her door had her jerking her head up. Bruce stood there, with that wide, dazzling smile just for her. He stepped inside, shut the door. "Here you are. I've been waiting for you."

She stared at him, saw her future as she'd envisioned it slipping away. This man loved her. For him to have to wait for her wasn't fair.

And she couldn't commit. Too many variables. Too many fears to conquer. She didn't want to be hurt again, to make the wrong choices with a man. There were too many steps forward that came with long slides back to a place only a tad farther than square one.

She couldn't put Bruce through that. Even here, she could tell he wanted to pull her into his arms and kiss her senseless. She wanted the same thing. But then, anyone could walk in. Everyone would know.

They'd watch with secretive little smiles, gossip over coffee cups.

Their relationship would overshadow everything in her life, especially the independence she was clinging to like a lifeline. She didn't want to live in anyone's shadow ever again, be only a Mrs. and not her own person.

"We can't see each other anymore," she blurted, and that smile vanished.

"What?"

"People know," she said simply. "That wasn't part of the deal. I want to be a lawyer in my own name. Maybe after the case. Maybe then…."

He shook his head. "Don't push me away, Christina. Don't do this again. I realize you're scared. We've talked about this."

"And you understand I must have time. We can't do this. We had a great night, but let's put it behind us. We have work to do, which we'll keep in the office from now on."

She'd slammed him sideways, and her own heart broke, proving perhaps how much she cared. *Just retract the words. Just throw yourself into his arms. Just believe.* But Christina couldn't.

Something held her back, a fear of something paralyzed her, and it was as if she were outside of her body as she listened to Bruce say, "If that's the way you want it, Christina. I only want you to be happy, and if this is what it takes…."

And then she watched helplessly as Bruce left her

office, closing the door with a decisive, final click. The world she wished she could have crashed to an end, not with a bang but with her own whimper of despair.

# Chapter Thirteen

When she finally had the courage to leave her office an hour later, the first person she ran into was Angela's temporary replacement, who quickly informed her that Bruce had left for Cyntech for the rest of the day.

"I didn't realize Bruce had more work left with Cyntech," Christina said.

"Something about a permit application," the temp replied. "Said he might not be back in the office until Monday. Said you'd handle the Title VII case and that he'd simply discuss it with you when he returned."

Meaning that he wasn't leaving any instructions for her, no reason for them to contact each other at all. He was giving her that space.

But this time, he wouldn't be present, not even in the same room and ignoring her. This time the break was permanent.

She wanted to cry, but instead, she squared her chin, went to the small conference room and sat down to work.

Concentration, however, was difficult. She could

picture Bruce in his familiar spot. She could almost smell his cologne. She'd run from Cincinnati, but she couldn't run from Morrisville. Bella was happy here. She would have to find a way to coexist with Bruce, and it wouldn't be easy.

"Mama, why are you sad?" Bella asked later that night after story time.

"Mama's just tired," Christina answered as she kissed Bella good-night. "It's hard getting back into a routine now that school's started again and we can't sleep in. So you get some rest. You're seeing your dad this weekend."

"He told me when he called that the Bengals would be in the Super Bowl."

"Maybe, just maybe," Christina said. She clicked the light off and went to her own room. Staring at her bed was painful. She and Bruce had tossed that comforter aside, rolled around on the sheets. She picked up a pillow. Even though she'd laundered everything, she could still smell his scent, still picture how he'd rested his head next to hers.

Leaving Kyle had been easier. She'd been angry. Determined not to take his infidelities any longer. The new had been a clean slate, a sidewalk washed by morning rain.

Now, even the bathroom adjacent to her bedroom was tainted. She and Bruce had showered together. He'd made love to her up against the counter. She could almost see him in the mirror, behind her, his eyes glazed with passion as he quickly thrust. She brushed her teeth, turned out the light and left the bathroom dark behind her.

She hadn't lied to Bella. She *was* tired. She had depositions to prepare for. A few more women to track down, as their cases had just come to light and thus they would become part of the suit. And Bruce wouldn't be around to help until Monday, and then, not like before.

Perhaps he was justified in taking himself out of the situation. She might have wanted to run, but she couldn't. She had to face the result of her fears. She'd given in to them and found failure. Didn't she also love to quote that other famous president: "The only thing we have to fear is fear itself"?

Franklin Delano Roosevelt had defined fear in his 1933 inaugural address as the "nameless, unreasoning, unjustified terror which paralyzes needed efforts to convert retreat into advance." He'd said the only thing you had to fear was fear itself.

Christina's fears had shut her down, ruined the best thing that had come along. She could hear Kyle's patronizing voice in her ear: "Christina Sanchez Jones, whenever will you learn?"

She had just learned that even though she'd graduated from Harvard, in the school of life she still had a lot of learning to do.

And the number-one thing would be how to mend a truly broken heart. Because she'd just comprehended that when you love someone and let him go because of your own fears of commitment and stupidity, you aren't protecting yourself. You're instead ripping a part of yourself out and throwing it away. Fear keeps you from even playing the game, much less winning.

And that hurt. Big-time.

LATE SUNDAY NIGHT Bruce was dreading Monday and his subsequent return to Lancaster and Morris, when the emergency fire call came that he was needed. He'd done everything that weekend to purge Christina from his mind—extra weight sets, extra work, extra fire duty—but she was still with him as he drove the fire truck, and still with him in the empty, burning restaurant that would be nothing but cinders when the fire was finally extinguished.

The icy wind whipped through the windows—the glass of Kim's Diner having exploded under pressure from the raging heat. The firemen worked desperately to keep the flames from jumping to the surrounding buildings, and then they labored to keep the building secure as it began to collapse.

Kim's, a popular breakfast and lunch eatery that closed daily at three, was about to become a smoldering ruin. The firefighters were ordered to leave the building and move to a safe perimeter.

The joist didn't necessarily catch Bruce at unawares, but it fell at such a freak angle that he had nowhere to go and no place to hide. Bruce's right arm rose to deflect the impending blow, but the heavy wayward beam grazed his helmet, tore at his right ear, landed on his shoulder and bounced off his elbow.

He winced as smoldering wood met bone, ripped through protective gear and met flesh. Then the pain fully exploded in his head, the oxygen mask skittered and the smoke blinded. Definitely time to get out. The falling beam had cost him valuable seconds.

He made to take a step and heard a sickening crack. The building was collapsing. As all hell rained down, his last thought was of Christina.

WHEN CHRISTINA DROVE into the Lancaster and Morris parking lot Monday morning, the first thing she noticed was the absence of Bruce's huge pickup truck. Not that this was odd. He'd been at Cyntech the previous week, after their altercation.

He was probably ignoring her some more, Christina thought as she exited her car, raced across the cold expanse and entered the heated building. Ten days into January, and any resolutions she'd had for a better year had bitten the dust.

The receptionist was on the phone, and Christina gave a quick wave as she passed by and entered the elevator. Angela's temporary replacement had already sorted the mail in Christina's in-box, and Christina cleared her mind and got to work.

A few hours later, a rapping at her door diverted her attention from the legal brief she'd been highlighting. She set down her marker and gazed up. Roy Lancaster stood in the doorway, resting his hands on his cane.

He shook his head. "Amazing. For once I see that you're actually in the office, exactly where you're supposed to be. And on a day when everyone else isn't."

Christina rolled her shoulders to stretch them. She tilted her head and glanced at the clock. She'd been sitting at her desk for over two hours. No wonder she was stiff. "Good morning, Roy. You see, I do work. And I don't have a meeting to be at this morning. As for no one else being here, I don't know anyone's schedule but mine."

"They're at the hospital," Roy announced. "Thought you'd be there."

"Did Angela have her baby?" Christina asked. "She was due a few days ago."

Roy tapped his cane on the floor as if buzzing her answer incorrect. "Do you not listen to the radio?"

"National Public Radio," Christina said. She really had no idea where he was going with this, but Roy could be eccentric. "And I read the *Wall Street Journal* every morning."

"Bah. Those big boys don't cover us. We're too rural and small town."

She stared at him, at a loss as to what to do. He'd made no move to enter her office. "Would you care to take a seat? I can get you some coffee."

"Not staying. Going back to the hospital. Maybe get something to eat."

"Is something wrong? Are you okay? I'm sure I can reach Bruce on his cell phone if you want to speak with him. I haven't seen him yet this morning."

Roy gazed past her, out one of Christina's windows. "Guess you don't have a view of Kim's from here."

"Kim's? The restaurant?" Christina had driven by it once or twice. What did that have to do with anything?

"Burned down last night," Roy said. "Nothing but rubble left. Word is Kim's going to rebuild, but that's of course after the insurance investigation. She's one of my former clients. I think Larry has her now. I always eat breakfast at Kim's."

"No one was hurt," Christina probed.

"Place was closed and empty."

"That's good," Christina said. She blinked. Roy was still standing and watching her, his gaze solemn. Then it hit her. He hadn't refuted her statement. "Roy?"

He shook his head, and fear unlike any Christina had ever experienced thundered through her like a runaway freight train. "Roy, what is going on? Why is everyone at the hospital? Was Bruce on call last night?"

Roy simply nodded, and Christina bolted to her feet. The case, her work—everything could wait. "I have to be there."

Roy nodded again. "Margaret Mary Community Hospital in Batesville. Cross back over the highway, make a right at the four-way stop and then a left. It's by the golf course. You can't miss it."

"Thank you."

As Christina flew out the door and into the unknown, Roy took a moment to survey her office and contemplate the events. By the time she got to the hospital, most everyone else would be gone. Really, no point anymore. Time to move on. Bruce would want that. Roy turned as he sensed another presence. Reginald Morris stood directly behind him. "Christina just went skittering into the elevator. I was coming up the stairs. Did you tell her?"

"I did. You saw how she took it."

"I did," Reginald said. Both he and Roy had already

been through enough in the past twelve hours, especially after Colin's early-morning confession in the hospital waiting room about Bruce's love life. "So what do you think she'll do?" Reginald asked. "When she realizes there's no—"

"Don't know," Roy interrupted. "But I'm not waiting around here to find out."

IT TOOK CHRISTINA twenty minutes to reach the hospital. She swore that had a policeman even tried to stop her for speeding, she probably would have strangled him, that was how worried and upset she was.

She raced up to the information desk, her low pumps clicking on the tile floor. The sign indicated visiting hours were in effect. "Bruce Lancaster's room," Christina said to the elderly receptionist, whose nametag proclaimed she'd been volunteering for twenty years.

"One moment," the woman replied.

Christina wanted to scream that she didn't have one moment. Instead she simply tapped her foot.

"Room 502," the woman told her. "He's...."

But Christina was already at the elevators, punching the buttons savagely. On the fifth floor she made a quick turn and found herself outside room 502. The door wasn't shut all the way and she could hear at least two voices coming from inside the room. One was Bruce's. Relief flowed. He was alive. The other was...female. That voice gave a low laugh. Christina listened a moment. The conversation was not that of a patient and a nurse.

A rage unlike she'd ever known overtook Christina. She felt as though she was inside a kaleidoscope. Past, present and future flashed by her eyes. Then suddenly the picture cleared, and Christina realized the absolute truth.

She loved Bruce Lancaster. Really loved him. He was her partner, the man she wanted to spend the rest of her life with. She'd been too blind, too fearful to acknowledge it until this moment.

The man had given her his heart, and she'd handed it back. She might have to use every weapon in her arsenal, but she was recapturing what was hers, what she couldn't live without any longer. And damn it, she didn't care who found out or who got in her way, including the woman inside.

Time was a precious commodity and she'd already wasted way too much of it. Christina Miranda Elise Sanchez Jones had finally learned.

She pushed the door wide, relieved the room was a private one. The occupants couldn't see her yet, not until she cleared the small hallway that led past the bathroom.

She stepped into view.

A woman sat in the chair next to Bruce, but Christina's gaze raked over her for placement purposes only. It was the man in the bed who commanded her attention. He wore a hospital gown, and the blankets and bed sheets covered him to mid chest. His right arm rested across his stomach, in a cast held with a dark-blue sling. His right ear was bandaged. No other tubes or wires jutted from his body; no monitors beeped. From what she could tell, he had at the minimum a broken arm and some cuts and scrapes.

Two sets of eyes turned toward her. A second passed before recognition dawned and Bruce realized she wasn't the nurse. "Christina."

She was as awkward as a girl on her first date. But she had newfound determination. "Bruce. Roy stopped by the office and told me you were here. You know how vague Roy can be. He made it sound like you were dying."

"That would be Roy," the woman said. "Mr. Exaggeration. Bruce, do you remember the time Roy…."

Christina ignored the story and studied the dark-haired woman. She had a fresh glow, as though she'd been outdoors recently.

"Your grandfather is correct about one thing, though," the woman in the chair stated. "He said this morning that it was time for you to leave the fire department. You've had your sign. I couldn't agree more."

"Christina," Bruce said gently, calling her attention back to him. A smile had tugged at his lips, as if he knew she was jealous. "Christina, I'd like you to meet my mother, Hannah Lancaster. She was just leaving."

"I am?" Bruce's mother blinked, but she stood in a moment straight out of a movie. "I'll stop by your house later tonight and check on you."

"I'll be fine," Bruce said. "I think Christina's going to be taking care of me. That is why you're here, isn't it?"

He'd thrown her the opening line she'd been waiting for. The man really didn't play games the way most men did. He'd never lied to her. Hope began to build. "Yes," Christina said. "I'm going to take care of him."

In the process of putting on her coat, Hannah Lancaster paused as though sensing something big was about to go down. Christina experienced her scrutiny, but she didn't hesitate in her quest. She faced Hannah. "He won't be going home," Christina told his mother. "He'll be at my place. I'll have to move his cat, but that's simpler than uprooting my daughter."

Hannah sputtered. "And…and you are?"

"The woman I plan to marry," Bruce said. "As soon as she agrees to have me, which is why you should go, Mom. I love you. Tell Dad I'll call him later, once they spring me."

"You're getting married," Hannah said. "We leave for a trip, barely return and—"

"Goodbye, Mom," Bruce called. "I'll explain everything. I promise. Right now I want to talk to Christina." He and Christina watched as Hannah left, mumbling.

"You deliberately drive that woman crazy, don't you?" Christina asked.

"Yeah," Bruce said. "But she always gets over it. She's my mom and she's finally getting what she's wanted. No more fire department. Your arrival saved me from her lecture. I've gotten it from everyone ever since visiting hours opened, and double from my family, who've been here all night. Come sit by me."

Concern laced her voice. "I don't want to hurt you."

"You won't. I have a broken arm and some bruises that'll take some time to heal, but the doctors are pretty certain I'll have no ill effects from the concussion I also suffered when the roof collapsed." He saw her pained expression. "Don't glare at me like that. They dug me out fast. I'm fine. This is minor."

"Your grandfather scared me to death." Christina gingerly sat down on the bed, and Bruce's left hand found hers. His touch held promise and warmth. "I thought something tragic had happened to you. I couldn't handle it," Christina admitted.

"I'm sorry about that. Scaring you was probably his intention. There was a little powwow this morning after Colin confessed that he'd paid you a visit Wednesday. I, of course, then had to say that we were finished. Kaput. Everyone knows our history. I realize you didn't want that."

"I don't care anymore," she said quickly. "The past doesn't matter one bit. The fact that you're okay, that we have another chance, is all that matters." She surveyed the hospital room. "We really don't have romantic environments, do we?"

He grinned, his smile lighting up his whole face. "I'll work on that in the future."

"Don't. Oddly, this seems somehow normal and right. Romance is what you make of it. It's not candles, flowers and everything else the greeting-card companies portray it to be, although those things are nice. But trinkets and flora aren't the keys to happiness, or I would have been deliriously happy with Kyle. No, it's what's in your heart that really counts, and that's where you won me over, Bruce. Your heart is solid gold, full of love and tenderness. You gave and gave to me without asking for anything. In return, I treated you terribly."

"Christina," he began.

But she wouldn't let him stop her. "I made a mistake, and I'm sorry. I never should have turned you away, never should have said those words that day. I was scared, but that doesn't make what I did right. However, I was more scared today when I thought I'd lost you. So I'm here to tell you that I'm putting on the boxing gloves for one more round. You have a piece of my heart, and I had a piece of yours. I want that piece back, and I'll fight for it if necessary. I love you, Bruce Lancaster, and I'm ready to shout it to the world."

"You are, huh?"

"You bet I am. You've never seen me determined."

The grin widened. "Really? You almost clocked me that first day."

"This will be much worse," she promised.

"We can't have that," he said. His tone turned serious. "I love you, Christina, and I want nothing more than to love you forever, even if it's on your terms."

"I've been thinking about those. I'm glad you want to marry me, because I've decided I'm going to insist on it."

He arched an eyebrow. "Is that a proposal?"

She nodded. "Oh, yes. It's the only solution to our problem. While I'm highly supportive of modern living arrangements, we don't want Morrisville's citizens all aghast over ours. And I think that for Bella's sake, I'd rather that any results of our, ah, liaison be, uh, legitimate. With the number of those, um, encounters, we'll have, I'm sure something might occur."

"All very valid points," Bruce said with a teasing nod. "I always wanted a large family."

Happiness made her smile. "Then we'll have to work on that, as hard as we're going to work on winning our case. After the legal proceedings are over, I'm planning on starting an organization to educate those women on their rights, so that something like this doesn't ever happen again."

"We will win it—I know we will. You're my equal, Christina, and together we can do anything. We have no limits."

"I've realized that. I love you. You make me complete. You complement me. I want nothing more than to be with you. With you, all things are possible."

"They are, darling. I love you." He paused, and then because she had no reply, Bruce asked, "So are you going to kiss me now?"

Christina blinked. From his expression, she could tell that Bruce was serious.

"I've been waiting since you got here to feel your lips on mine," he continued. "The instant you walked in the door I hoped I knew why you were here. But it didn't matter whether I was right. I was going to come after you the moment they released me, and no amount of argument would have swayed me. You were the last thought in my mind when the roof caved in. Time is too valuable to waste."

"It is," she said.

"Then kiss me, my sweetheart."

She smiled as a love that knew no bounds increased exponentially. This was her man, her future, her life. She'd found her heart's desire. Heaven waited.

"Only if you promise me one thing," she whispered as she lowered her mouth to his.

"What's that?" he asked, shifting to better reach her.

"Once you kiss me, you can never let me go."

"Promise made, my love. Are you ready for that kiss?"

She was. Nothing held her back anymore. No fear. No indecision. Whatever problems she and Bruce might face, they would face them together. She'd saved herself, and managed to get the castle and the prince, as well. "I love you," she said.

"Good," Bruce said. His lips touched hers, stamping Case Closed on their past. "I love you, too, Christina. My darling, my heart."

Then, with a long tender kiss of love that sent her spiraling, Bruce settled any doubt once and forever and opened a new file, the one that would be their future.

Christina knew she'd finally come home, and while her life might not ever be perfectly normal, life was finally good.

*American* **ROMANCE**®

## Motherhood

**Motherhood: what it
means to raise a child.**

# THE BABY
# INHERITANCE
### by Ann Roth
#### American Romance #1103

When Mia Barker learns she has been named
legal guardian of a relative's baby, she finds
herself in a state of shock. Running a vet clinic
and taking care of animals is one thing, but with
a painful event from her past still haunting her,
she doesn't feel capable of raising a child. Can
Hank Adams convince Mia to let baby
Drew—and him—into her heart?

*Available February 2006
wherever Harlequin books are sold.*

# *American* | ROMANCE®

## A THREE-BOOK SERIES BY
# Kaitlyn Rice

## Heartland Sisters

*To the folks in Augusta, Kansas, the three sisters were the Blume girls—a little pitiable, a bit mysterious and different enough to be feared.*

*The three sisters may have received an odd upbringing, but there's nothing odd about the affection, esteem and support they have for one another, no matter what crises come their way.*

# THE RUNAWAY BRIDESMAID

When Isabel Blume catches the bridal bouquet at a friend's wedding, and realizes her long-standing boyfriend has no intention of marrying her, she heads off to spend the summer at a friend's Colorado wilderness camp. There she meets the man whose proposal she really wants to hear. So why does she refuse him?

### Available February 2006

## Also look for:
# THE LATE BLOOMER'S BABY
### Available October 2005

# THE THIRD DAUGHTER'S WISH
### Available June 2006

*Available wherever Harlequin books are sold.*

## *American* ROMANCE®

**IS DELIGHTED TO BRING YOU FOUR NEW
BOOKS IN A MINISERIES BY POPULAR AUTHOR**

# Jacqueline Diamond

### Downhome Doctors
*First-rate doctors
in a town of second chances.*

## NINE-MONTH SURPRISE
### On sale February 2006

First-grade teacher Leah Morris gives in to temptation
and allows herself a fling with a dream man. What
happens next brings as many surprises as she and
Dr. Will Rankin—the new physician at the Downhome,
Tennessee, medical clinic and recently divorced father
of six-year-old twin girls—can ever imagine.

Also look for:
### THE POLICE CHIEF'S LADY
### On sale December 2005

### A FAMILY AT LAST
### On sale April 2006

### DAD BY DEFAULT
### On sale June 2006

*Available wherever Harlequin books are sold.*

**www.eHarlequin.com**     HARJDMFEB

## SHOWCASING...

*New York Times* bestselling author

# JOAN HOHL

## HOME TO LOVE

**A classic story about two people
who finally discover great love....**

"Ms. Hohl always creates a vibrant ambiance
to capture our fancy."
—*Romantic Times*

**Coming in February.**

**A breathtaking novel of
reunion and romance...**

## Once a Rebel

### by Sheri WhiteFeather

Returning home to Red Rock after many
years, psychologist Susan Fortune is reunited
with Ethan Eldridge, a man she hasn't gotten
over in seventeen years. When tragedy and grief
overtake the family, Susan leans on Ethan to
overcome her feelings—and soon realizes that
her life can't be complete without him.

**Coming in February**